"We're going

"The best," he ... ut the wedding expe... going to pay for everything."

"You don't have to do that."

"I want to." He touched her cheek, then lifted his hand away. "But what am I going to do during the part of the ceremony where I'm supposed to kiss my bride?"

She wet her lips, a bit too quickly. "You'll have to kiss her, I guess."

"She's going to have to kiss me back, too."

Her pulse fluttered at her neck, as soft as a butterfly, as sexy as a summer breeze. "Yes, she will."

As they both fell silent, she glanced away, trapped in feelings she couldn't seem to control. She didn't want to imagine what the wedding kiss was going to be like.

Still, she wondered how it would unfold. Would he whisper something soft and soothing before he leaned into her? Would their mouths be slightly open, their eyes completely closed? Would she sigh and melt against him, like a princess being awakened by the wrong prince?

Just thinking about it felt forbidden.

* * *

Paper Wedding, Best-Friend Bride is part of the Billionaire Brothers Club series—

Three foster brothers grow up, get rich...and find the perfect woman.

Dear Reader,

I've been involved in small, intimate weddings, but I've never experienced the wonderful, wild, crazy, stressful adventure of planning a big ceremony. Of course, I've planned and created lots of different types of weddings for the characters in my books.

This story contains a whirlwind high-society wedding. Mostly I enjoyed choosing the dress and the wedding colors. The flowers, too, since they were part of a special garden that was planted for the occasion. Oh, and the rings. That was a fascinating and highly significant aspect, as well.

Also, there is quite a bit of symbolism related to the wedding in this book. You'll know what I mean when you come across those portions in the plot.

I would love to hear from you about your wedding or any other weddings that you helped plan. Were you the bride, maid of honor, a bridesmaid or the mother of the bride? What styles of dresses did the bride and bridesmaids wear? What were the colors? Did you use a wedding planner or did you do it all on your own? In what season did the ceremony take place? What type of reception was arranged? Tell me all of it! I want to know, as I'm certain that I will be planning more "book" weddings in the future.

Love and Hugs,

Sheri WhiteFeather

SHERI WHITEFEATHER

PAPER WEDDING, BEST-FRIEND BRIDE

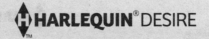

Recycling programs
for this product may
not exist in your area.

ISBN-13: 978-0-373-83835-6

Paper Wedding, Best-Friend Bride

Copyright © 2017 by Sheree Henry-Whitefeather

Printed in U.S.A.

Sheri WhiteFeather is an award-winning, bestselling author. She writes a variety of romance novels for Harlequin and is known for incorporating Native American elements into her stories. She has two grown children, who are tribally enrolled members of the Muscogee Creek Nation. She lives in California and enjoys shopping in vintage stores and visiting art galleries and museums. Sheri loves to hear from her readers at sheriwhitefeather.com.

Books by Sheri WhiteFeather

Harlequin Desire

Marriage of Revenge
The Morning-After Proposal

Billionaire Brothers Club

Waking Up with the Boss
Single Mom, Billionaire Boss
Paper Wedding, Best-Friend Bride

Harlequin Special Edition

Family Renewal

The Bachelor's Baby Dilemma
Lost and Found Husband
Lost and Found Father

Visit her Author Profile page at Harlequin.com, or sheriwhitefeather.com, for more titles.

One

Lizzie McQueen emerged from a graceful dip in Max Marquez's black-bottom pool, water glistening on her bikini-clad body.

Reminiscent of a slow-motion scene depicted in a movie, she stepped onto the pavement and reached for a towel, and he watched every long-legged move she made. While she dried herself off, he swigged his root beer and pretended that he wasn't checking out her perfectly formed cleavage or gold pierced navel or—

"Come on, Max, quit giving me *the look*."

Caught in the act, he dribbled the stupid drink down his chin. She shook her head and tossed him her towel. He cursed beneath his breath and wiped his face.

The look was code for when either of them ogled the other in an inappropriate manner. They'd agreed quite a while ago that sex, or anything that could possibly lead to it, was off the table. They cared too much about each other to ruin their friendship with a few deliciously hot romps in the sack. Even now, at thirty years old, they held a platonic promise between them.

She smoothed back her fiery red hair, placed a big, floppy hat on her head and stretched out on the chaise next to him. Max lived in a 1930s Beachwood Canyon mansion, and Lizzie resided in an ultra-modern condo. She spent more time at his place than he did at hers because he preferred it that way. His Los Angeles lair was bigger, badder and much more private.

He returned the towel, only now it had his soda stain on it. She rolled her eyes, and they shared a companionable grin.

He handed her a bottle of sunscreen. "You better reapply this."

She sighed. "Me and my sensitive skin."

He liked her ivory complexion. But he'd seen her get some nasty sunburns, too. He didn't envy her that. She slathered on the lotion, and he considered how they'd met during their senior year in high school. They were being paired up on a chemistry project, and, even then, she'd struck him as a debutant-type girl.

Later he'd learned that she was originally from Savannah, Georgia, with ties to old money. In that regard, his assessment of her had been correct, and just being near her had sent his boyhood longings into a tailspin. Not only was she gorgeous; she was everything he'd wanted to be: rich, prestigious, popular.

But Max had bottomed out on the other end of the spectrum: a skinny, dorky Native American foster kid with a genius IQ and gawky social skills, leaving him open to scorn and ridicule.

Of course, Lizzie's life hadn't been as charmed as he'd assumed it was. Once he'd gotten to know her, she'd revealed her deepest, darkest secrets to him, just as he'd told her his.

Supposedly during that time, when they were pouring their angst-riddled hearts out to each other, she'd actually formed a bit of a crush on him. But even till this day, he found that hard to fathom. In what alternate universe did prom queens get infatuated with dorks?

She peered at him from beneath the fashionable brim of her pale beige hat. Her bathing suit was a shimmering shade of copper with a leopard-print trim, and her meticulously manicured nails were painted a soft warm pink. Every lovely thing about her purred, "trust fund heiress," which was exactly what she was.

"What are you thinking about?" she asked.

He casually answered, "What a nerd I used to be."

She teased him with a smile. "As opposed to the sexy billionaire you are today?"

"Right." He laughed a little. "Because nothing

says beefcake like a software designer and internet entrepreneur."

She moved her gaze along the muscle-whipped length of his body. "You've done all right for yourself."

He raised his eyebrows. "Now who's giving who *the look*?"

She shrugged off her offense. "You shouldn't have become such a hottie if you didn't want to get noticed."

That wasn't the reason he'd bulked up, and she darned well knew it. Sure, he'd wanted to shed his nerdy image, but he'd started hitting the gym after high school for more than aesthetic purposes. His favorite sport was boxing. Sometimes he shadowboxed and sometimes he pounded the crap out of a heavy bag. But mostly he did it to try to pummel the demons that plagued him. He was a runner, too. So was Lizzie. They ran like a tornado was chasing them. Or their pasts, which was pretty much the same thing.

"Beauty and the brainiac," he said. "We were such a teenage cliché."

"Why, because you offered to tutor me when I needed it? That doesn't make us a cliché. Without your help, I would never have gotten my grades up to par or attended my mother's alma mater."

Silent, Max nodded. She'd also been accepted into her mom's old sorority, which had been another of her goals. But none of that had brought her the comfort she'd sought.

"The twentieth anniversary is coming up," she said.

Of her mom's suicide, he thought. Lizzie was ten when her high-society mother had swallowed an entire bottle of sleeping pills. "I'm sorry you keep reliving it." She mentioned it every year around this time, and even now he could see her childhood pain.

She put the sunscreen aside, placing it on a side table, where her untouched iced tea sat. "I wish I could forget about her."

"I know." He couldn't get his mom out of his head, either, especially the day she'd abandoned him, leaving him alone in their run-down apartment. He was eight years old, and she'd parked him in front of the TV, warning him to stay there until she got back. She was only supposed to be gone for a few hours, just long enough to score the crack she routinely smoked. Max waited for her return, but she never showed up. Scared out of his young mind, he'd fended for himself for three whole days, until he'd gone to a neighbor for help. "My memories will probably never stop haunting me, either."

"We do have our issues."

"Yeah, we do." Max was rescued and placed in foster care, and a warrant was issued for his mom's arrest. But she'd already hit the road with her latest loser boyfriend, where she'd partied too hard and overdosed before the police caught up with her.

"What would you say to your mother if she was still alive?" Lizzie asked.

"Nothing."

"You wouldn't tell her off?"

"No." He wouldn't say a single word to her.

"You wouldn't even ask her why she used to hurt you?"

Max shook his head. There wasn't an answer in the world that would make sense, so what would be the point? When Mom hadn't been kicking him with her cheap high heels or smacking him around, she'd taken to burning him with cigarette butts and daring him not to cry. But her most common form of punishment was locking him in his closet, where she'd told him that the Lakota two-faced monsters dwelled.

The legends about these humanoid creatures varied. In some tales, it was a woman who'd been turned into this type of being after trying to seduce the sun god. One of her faces was beautiful, while the other was hideous. In other stories, it was a man with a second face on the back of his head. Making eye contact with him would get you tortured and killed. Cannibalism and kidnapping were among his misdeeds, too, with a malevolent glee for preying on misbehaving children.

The hours Max had spent in his darkened closet, cowering from the monsters and praying for his drugged-out mother to remove the chair that barred the door, would never go away.

He cleared his throat and said, "Mom's worst crime was her insistence that she loved me. But you already know all this." He polished off the last of his root beer and crushed the can between his palms, squeezing the aluminum down to nearly nothing. He repeated another thing she already knew. "I swear,

I never want to hear another woman say that to me again."

"I could do without someone saying that to me, too. Sure, love is supposed to be the cure-all, but not for…"

"People like us?"

She nodded, and he thought about how they tumbled in and out of affairs. Max went through his lovers like wine. Lizzie wasn't any better. She didn't get attached to her bedmates, either.

"At least I have my charity work," she said.

He was heavily involved in nonprofits, too, with it being a significant part of his life. "Do you think it's enough?"

"What?" She raised her delicately arched brows. "Helping other people? Of course it is."

"Then why am I still so dissatisfied?" He paused to study the sparkling blue of her eyes and the way her hair was curling in damp waves around her shoulders. "And why are you still stressing over your mom's anniversary?"

She picked up her tea, sipped, put it back down. "We're only human."

"I know. But I should be ashamed of myself for feeling this way. I got everything I ever wanted. I mean, seriously, look at this place." He scowled at his opulent surroundings. How rich and privileged and spoiled could he be?

"I thought your sabbatical helped." She seemed to be evaluating how long he'd been gone, separating himself from her and everyone else.

He'd taken nearly a year off to travel the world, to search for inner peace. He'd also visited hospitals and orphanages and places where he'd hoped to make a difference. "The most significant part of that experience was the months I spent in Nulah. It's a small island country in the South Pacific. I'd never been there before, so I didn't really know what to expect. Anyway, what affected me was this kid I came across in an orphanage there. A five-year-old boy named Tokoni."

She cocked her head. "Why haven't you mentioned him before now?"

"I don't know." He conjured up an image of the child's big brown eyes and dazzling smile. "Maybe I was trying to keep him to myself a little longer and imagine him with the family his mother wanted him to have. When he was two, she left him at the orphanage, hoping that someone would adopt him and give him a better life. She wasn't abusive to him, like my mother was to me. She just knew that she couldn't take proper care of him. Nulah is traditional in some areas, with old-world views, and rough and dangerous in others. It didn't used to be so divided, but it started suffering from outside influences."

"Like drugs and prostitution and those sorts of things?"

"Yes, and Tokoni's mother lived in a seedy part of town and was struggling to find work. She'd already lost her family in a boating accident, so there was no one left to help her."

"What about the boy's father?" she asked. "How does he fit into this?"

"He was an American tourist who made all sorts of promises, saying he was going to bring her to the States and marry her. But in the end, he didn't do anything, except ditch her and the kid."

"Oh, how awful." Lizzie's voice broke a little. "That makes me sad for her, living on a shattered dream, waiting for a man to whisk her away."

It disturbed Max, too. "She kept in touch with the orphanage for a while, waiting to see if Tokoni ever got a permanent home, but then she caught pneumonia and died. The old lady who operates the place told me the story. It's a private facility that survives on charity. I already donated a sizable amount to help keep them on track."

She made a thoughtful expression. "I can write an article about them to drum up more support, if you want."

"That would be great." Max appreciated the offer. Lizzie hosted a successful philanthropy blog with tons of noble-hearted followers. "I just wish someone would adopt Tokoni. He's the coolest kid, so happy all the time." So different from how Max was as a child. "He's at the age where he talks about getting adopted and thinks it's going to happen. He's been working on this little picture book, with drawings of the mommy and daddy he's convinced he's going to have. They're just stick figures with smiley faces, but to him, they're real."

"Oh, my goodness." She tapped a hand against her heart. "That's so sweet."

"He's a sweet kid. I've been wanting to return to the island to see him again. Just to let him know that I haven't forgotten about him."

"Then you should plan another trip soon."

"Yeah, I should." Max could easily rearrange his schedule to make it happen. "Hey, here's an idea. Do you want to come to Nulah with me to meet him?" He suspected that Lizzie could manage her time to accommodate a trip, as well. She'd always been a bit of a jet-setter, a spontaneous society girl ready to leave town on a whim. But mostly she traveled for humanitarian causes, so this was right up her alley. "While we're there, you can interview the woman who operates the orphanage for the feature you're going to do on your blog."

"Sure. I can go with you. I'd like to see the orphanage and conduct an in-person interview. But I should probably spend most of my time with her and let you visit with Tokoni on your own. You know how kids never really take to me."

"You just need to relax around them." Although Lizzie championed hundreds of children's charities, she'd never gotten the gist of communicating with kids, especially the younger ones. A side effect from her own youth, he thought, from losing her mom and forcing herself to grow up too fast. "For the record, I think you and Tokoni will hit it off just fine. In fact, I think he's going to be impressed with you."

"You do?" She adjusted her lounge chair, moving it to a more upright position. "What makes you say that?"

"In his culture redheads are said to descend from nobility, from a goddess ruler who dances with fire, and your hair is as bright as it gets." Max sat forward, too, and leaned toward her. "He'll probably think you're a princess or something. But you were homecoming queen. So it's not as if you didn't have your reign."

Her response fell flat. "That doesn't count."

He remembered going to the football game that night, sitting alone in the bleachers, watching her receive her crown. He'd skipped the homecoming dance. He wouldn't have been able to blend in there. Getting a date would have been difficult, too. As for Lizzie, she'd attended the dance with the tall, tanned star of the boys' swim team. "It counted back then."

"Not to me, not like it should have. It wasn't fair that my other friends didn't accept you."

"Well, I got the last laugh, didn't I?"

She nodded, even if neither of them was laughing.

Before things got too morose, he reached out and tugged on a strand of her hair. "Don't fret about being royalty to me. The only redhead that influenced my culture was a woodpecker."

She sputtered into a laugh and slapped his hand away. "Gee, thanks, for that compelling tidbit."

He smiled, pleased by her reaction. "It's one of those old American Indian tales. I told it to Tokoni when he was putting a puzzle together with pictures of birds." Max stopped smiling. "The original story involves love. But I left off that part when I told To-koni. I figured he was too young to understand it. Plus, it would have been hypocritical of me to tell it that way."

She took a ladylike sip of her tea. "Now I'm curious about the original version and just how lovey-dovey it is."

"It's pretty typical, I guess." He went ahead and recited it, even if he preferred it without the romance. "It's about a hunter who loves a girl from his village, but she's never even noticed him. He thinks about her all the time. He even has trouble sleeping because he can't get her off his mind. So he goes to the forest to be alone, where he hears a beautiful song that lulls him to sleep. That night, he dreams about a woodpecker who says, 'Follow me and I'll show you how to make this song.' In the morning, he sees a real woodpecker and follows him. The bird is tapping on a branch and the familiar song is coming from it. Later, the hunter returns home with the branch and tries to make the music by waving it in the air, but it doesn't work."

Lizzie removed her hat. By now the sun was shifting in the sky, moving behind the trees and dappling her in scattered light. But mostly what Max noticed was how intense she looked, listening to the silly myth. Or was her intensity coming from the energy that always seemed to dance between them? The sexiness that seeped through their pores?

Ignoring the feeling, he continued by saying, "The hunter has another dream where the woodpecker shows him how to blow on the wood and tap the holes to make the song he'd first heard. Obviously, it's a flute the bird made. But neither the hunter nor his people had ever seen this type of instrument before."

She squinted at him. "What happens with the girl?"

"Once she hears the hunter's beautiful song, she looks into his eyes and falls in love with him, just as he'd always loved her. But like I said, I told it to Tokoni without the romance."

She was still squinting, intensity still etched on her face. "Where did you first come across this story? Was it in one of the books you used to read?"

"Yes." When he was in foster care, he'd researched his culture, hoping to find something good in it. "I hated that the only thing my mom ever talked about was the scary stuff. But I'm glad that Tokoni's mother tried to do right by him."

"Me, too." She spoke softly. "Parents are supposed to want what's best for their children."

He met her gaze, and she stared back at him, almost like the girl in the hunter's tale—except that love didn't appeal to either of them.

But desire did. If Lizzie wasn't his best friend, if she was someone he could kiss without consequence, he would lock lips with her right now, pulling her as close to him as he possibly could. And with the way she was looking at him, she would probably let him kiss the hell out of her. But that wouldn't do either of them any good.

"I appreciate you coming to Nulah with me," he said, trying to shake off the heat of wanting her. "It means a lot to me, having you there."

"I know it does," she replied, reaching for his hand.

But it was only the slightest touch. She pulled away quickly. Determined, it seemed, to control her hunger for him, too.

A myriad of thoughts skittered through Lizzie's mind. Today she and Max were leaving on their trip, and she should be done packing, as he would be arriving soon to pick her up. Yet she was still sorting haphazardly through her clothes and placing them in her suitcase. Normally Lizzie was far more organized. But for now she couldn't think clearly.

She hated it when her attraction to Max dragged her under its unwelcome spell, and lately it seemed to be getting worse. But they'd both learned to deal with it, just as she was trying to get a handle on how his attachment to Tokoni was making her feel. Even with his troubled past, being around children was easy for Max. Lizzie was terribly nervous about meeting the boy. Kids didn't relate to her in the fun-and-free way they did with him. Of course her stodgy behavior in their presence didn't help. But no matter how hard she tried, she couldn't seem to change that side of herself.

After her mother had drifted into a deathly sleep, she'd compensated for the loss by taking on the characteristics of an adult, long before she should have.

But what choice did she have? Her grieving father had bailed out on parenthood, leaving her with nannies and cooks. He'd immersed himself in his high-powered work and business travels, allowing her to grow up in a big lonely house full of strangers. Lizzie didn't have any extended family to speak of.

Even after all these years, she and her dad barely communicated. Was it any wonder that she'd gone off to Columbia University searching for a connection to her mom? She'd even taken the same journalism major. She'd walked in her mother's path, but it hadn't done a bit of good. She'd returned with the same disjointed feelings.

Her memories of her mom were painfully odd: scattered images of a beautifully fragile blonde who used to stare unblinkingly at herself in the mirror, who used to give lavish parties and tell Lizzie how essential it was for a young lady of her standing to be a good hostess, who used to laugh at the drop of a hat and then cry just as easily. Mama's biggest ambition was to be awarded the Pulitzer Prize. But mostly she just threw away her writings. Sometimes she even burned them, tossing them into the fireplace and murmuring to herself in French, the language of her ancestors.

Mama was rife with strange emotions, with crazy behaviors, but she was warm and loving, too, cuddling Lizzie at night. Without her sweet, dreamy mother by her side, Elizabeth "Lizzie" McQueen had been crushed, like a bug on a long white limousine's windshield.

After Mama killed herself, Dad sold their Savannah home, got a new job in Los Angeles and told Lizzie that she was going to be a California kid from then on.

But by that time she'd already gotten used to imitating her mother's lady-of-the-manor ways, presenting a rich-girl image that made her popular. Nonetheless, she'd lied to her new friends, saying that her socialite mother had suffered a brain aneurysm. Dad told his new workmates the same phony story. Lizzie had been coaxed by him to protect their privacy, and she'd embraced the lie.

Until she met Max.

She'd felt compelled to reveal the truth to him. But he was different from her other peers—a shy, lonely boy, who was as damaged as she was.

The doorbell rang, and Lizzie caught her breath.

She dashed to answer the summons, and there he was: Max Marquez, with his longish black hair shining like a raven's wing. He wore it parted down the middle and falling past his neck, but not quite to his shoulders. His deeply set eyes were brown, but sometimes they looked as black as his hair. His face was strong and angular, with a bone structure to die for. The gangly teenager he'd once been was gone. He'd grown into a fiercely handsome man.

"Are you ready?" he asked.

She shook her head. "Sorry. No. I'm still packing."

He entered her condo. "That's okay. I'll text my pilot and tell him we're running late."

Lizzie nodded. Max's success provided him the

luxury of a private jet. She'd inherited her mother's old Savannah money, but she was nowhere as wealthy as he was. He wasn't the only Native American foster kid in LA who'd made good. He remained close to two of his foster brothers, who'd also become billionaires. Max had been instrumental in helping them attain their fortunes, loaning them money to get their businesses off the ground.

He followed her into her room, where her suitcase was on the bed, surrounded by the clothes she'd been sorting.

He lifted a floral-printed dress from the pile. "This is pretty." He glanced at a lace bra and panty set. "And those." Clearly, he was teasing her, as if making a joke was easier than anything else he could think of doing or saying.

"Knock it off." She grabbed the lingerie and shoved them into a pouch on the side of her Louis Vuitton luggage, glad that he hadn't actually touched her underwear. As for the dress, she tugged it away from him.

"Did you really have a thing for me in high school?" he asked.

Oh, goodness. He was bringing that up now? "Yes, I really did." She'd developed a quirky little crush on him, formed within the ache of the secrets they'd shared. But he'd totally blown her away when she returned from university and saw his physical transformation. He'd changed in all sorts of ways by then. While she'd been hitting the books, he'd already earned his first million, selling an app he'd designed, and he hadn't even gone to college. These days, he invested in start-ups and made a killing doing it.

"It never would have worked between us," he said.

Lizzie considered flinging her makeup bag at him and knocking him upside that computer chip brain of his. "I never proposed that it would."

"You were too classy for me." He gazed at her from across the bed. "Sometimes I think you still are."

A surge of heat shot through her blood. "That's nonsense. You date tons of socialites. They're your type."

"Because you set the standard. How could I be around you and not want that type?"

"Don't do this, Max." He'd gone beyond the realm of making jokes. "You shouldn't even be in my room, let alone be saying that sort of stuff."

"As if." He brushed it off. "I've been in your room plenty of times before. Remember last New Year's Eve? I poured you into bed when you got too drunk to stand."

She looked at him as if he'd gone mad. But maybe he had lost his grip on reality. Or maybe she had. Either way, she challenged him. "What are you talking about? I wasn't inebriated. I was coming down with the flu."

"So you kept telling me." He gave her a pointed look. "I think it was all those cosmopolitans that international playboy lover of yours kept plying you with."

Seriously? His memory couldn't be that bad. "You were tending bar at the party that night." Here at her house, with her guests.

"Was I? Are you sure? I thought it was that Grand Prix driver you met in Monte Carlo. The one all the women swooned over."

"He and I were over by then." She wagged a finger at him. "You're the one who kept adding extra vodka to my drinks."

"I must have felt sorry for you, getting dumped by that guy."

"From what I recall, it was around the same time that department store heiress walked out on you."

"She was boring, anyway."

"I thought she was nice. She was hunting for a husband, though."

"Yeah, and that ruled me out. I wouldn't get married if the survival of the world depended on it."

"Me, neither. But what's the likelihood of us ever having to do that, for saving mankind or any other reason?"

"There isn't. But I still say that you were drunk last New Year's, and I was the gentleman—thank you very much—who tucked you into this very bed." He patted her pillow for effect, putting a dent in it.

"Oh, there's an oxymoron. The guy feeding me liquor is the gentleman in the story?"

"It beats your big-fish tale about having the flu."

"Okay. Fine. I was wasted. Now stop taking it out on my pillow."

"Oops, sorry." He plumped it back up, good as

new. "Are you going to finish packing or we going to sit here all day, annoying each other?"

"You started it." She filled her suitcase, stuffing it to the gills. She only wished they were going on a trip that didn't include a child she was nervous about meeting.

"Are you still worried about whether or not Tokoni will like you?" he asked, homing in on her troubled expression. "I already told you that I think you're going to impress him."

"Because he might regard me as a princess? That feels like pressure in itself."

"It'll be all right, Lizzie. And I promise, once you meet him, you'll see how special he is."

She didn't doubt that Tokoni was a nice little boy. But that didn't ease her nerves or boost her confidence about meeting him. Of course for now all she could do was remain by Max's side, supporting his cause, like the friend she was meant to be.

Two

Lizzie awakened inside a bungalow, with a tropical breeze stirring through an open window. Alone with her thoughts, she sat up and stretched.

Yesterday afternoon she and Max had arrived at their destination and checked in to the resort he'd booked for their weeklong stay. They had separate accommodations, each with its own colorful garden and oceanfront deck, equipped with everything they needed to relax, including hammocks. The interiors were also decorated to complement the environment, with beamed ceilings, wood floors, cozy couches and canopy beds.

Nulah consisted of a series of islands, and the sparsely populated island they were on was a twenty-minute boat ride to the mainland, the main island within the nation, where the capital city and all the activities in that area were: the airport, the orphanage they would be visiting, shopping and dining, dance clubs and other tourist-generated nightlife, nice hotels, cheap motels, burgeoning crime, basically what you would find in any city except on a smaller scale.

Of course at this off-the-grid resort, things were quiet. Max had stayed here before, during his sabbatical, and now Lizzie understood why it appealed to him.

With another body-rolling stretch, she climbed out of bed. She suspected that Max was already wide awake and jogging along the beach. He preferred early-morning runs. Typically, Lizzie did, too. But she'd skipped that routine today.

She showered and fixed her makeup and hair, keeping it simple. She didn't want to show up at the orphanage looking like a spoiled heiress. Or a princess. Or anything that drew too much attention to herself.

Returning to her bedroom, she donned the floral-printed dress Max had manhandled when she was packing yesterday, pairing it with T-strap sandals.

Lizzie made a cup of coffee, with extra cream, and headed outside. With a quiet sigh, she settled into a chair on her deck and gazed out at the view—the pearly white sand and aqua-blue water.

She closed her eyes, and when she opened them, Max appeared along the shore, winding down from his run. For a moment, he almost seemed like an apparition, a tall, tanned warrior in the morning light.

He glanced in her direction, and she waved him over. But before he strode toward her, he stopped to remove his T-shirt, using it like a towel to dry the sweat from his face and chest. Lizzie got a sexy little pulse-palpitating reaction from watching him. He'd already told her that his shower was outside, located in a walled section of his garden. He'd requested a bungalow with that type of amenity. So now she was going to envision him, naked in the elements, with water streaming over his sun-bronzed skin.

"Hey." He stood beside her chair. "What happened? I was expecting to see you out there. I figured you would've joined me at some point."

"I wasn't in the mood to run today." She glanced past him, making sure that she wasn't ogling his abs or giving him *the look*. Instead, she checked out a foamy wave breaking onto the shore. This island was a certified marine reserve, allowing guests to snorkel off the beach from the front of their bungalows. Lizzie hadn't been in the ocean yet, but according to Max there were heaps of fish, clams and coral reefs.

"You look pretty," he said.

His compliment gave her pulse another little jump start, prompting her to meet his gaze. "Thank you."

"I like your hair that way."

All she'd done was tie a satin ribbon around a carefully fastened ponytail, creating a girlish bow. "It's nothing, really."

"I think it gives you an interesting quality. Like a socialite trying to be incognito."

So much for her plan to be less noticeable. She

changed the subject. "You must be hungry by now. I can get us something and bring it back here." Although room service was available, there was also an eat-in or takeout breakfast buffet. She didn't mind packing up their food to go. The restaurant and bar that provided their meals was a short walk along the beach.

She waited while he balled up his sweaty T-shirt and pondered her suggestion.

Finally he said, "I'll take bacon and eggs and a large tumbler of orange juice. Last time I was here, they served seafood crepes in this mouthwatering wine-cheese sauce, so fill my plate with those, too. I'm pretty sure they'll have them again. It's one of their specialties."

Apparently he'd worked up an appetite. "Anything else?"

"No. But I have to shower first."

Damn, she thought. The outdoor shower she shouldn't be thinking about. "Go ahead, and I'll see you in a few."

He left, and she watched him until he was out of sight. She finished her coffee, then headed for the buffet.

As she made the picturesque trek, she admired the purple and pink flowers she passed along the way. They flourished on abundant vines, growing wild in the sandy soil. The garden attached to her bungalow was also filled with them, along with big leafy plants and tall twisty palms.

After she got their food, she set everything up

on her patio table. Inspired by the flora that surrounded her, she used a live orchid from her room as the centerpiece.

Max returned wearing a Polynesian-print shirt, board shorts and flip-flops. His thick damp hair was combed away from his face, but it was already starting to part naturally on its own. He smelled fresh and masculine, like the sandalwood soap he favored. Lizzie had used the mango-scented body wash the resort gave them.

He said, "This looks good." He sat across from her and dived into his big hearty breakfast.

For herself, she'd gotten plain yogurt and a bowl of fresh-cut fruit. But she hadn't been able to resist the crepes, so she was indulging in them, too.

He glanced up from his plate and asked, "Do you want to see a picture of Tokoni? I meant to show it to you before now. It's of the two of us."

"Yes, of course." She waited for him to pull it up on his phone, which took all of a second.

He handed it to her. The photo was of an adorable little dark-haired, tanned-skinned boy, expressing a big toothy grin. Max looked happy in the picture, too. She surmised that it was a selfie, snapped at close range. "He's beautiful."

"He's smart as a whip, too. Kindergarten starts at six here, so he isn't in school yet. But they work with the younger ones at the orphanage, preparing them for it." He took the phone back and set it aside. "I'm glad that you'll get to meet him today."

"What time are we supposed to be there?"

"We don't have an appointment. Losa said we can come any time it's convenient for us."

"That's her name? Losa? The woman who runs the orphanage?" The lady Lizzie would be interviewing today.

He nodded. "The kids call her Mrs. Losa."

"So is that her first or last name?"

"Her first. It means Rose in their native tongue."

That seemed fitting, with all the other flowers Lizzie had encountered today. "Is there a mister? Is she married?"

"She's widowed. She started the orphanage after her husband died. They were together for nearly forty years before he passed away."

She couldn't imagine being with the same person all that time. Or losing him.

"She has five kids," Max said. "They had three of their own, but they also adopted two from their village, orphaned siblings whose extended family wasn't able to care for them. But those children weren't adopted in an official way. Losa and her husband just took them in and raised them."

"Really? That's legal here?"

"Yes, but mostly it's the country folks, the traditionalists who still do that. They live in small communities where the people are tightly knit, so if there's a child or children in need, they band together to help. Losa and her husband used to be farmers. But she sold her property and moved to the capital to open the orphanage when she learned how many kids on the mainland were homeless. Her entire family supported her decision and relocated with her. All of her children and their spouses work there, along with their kids. She has two grown granddaughters and three teenage grandsons."

"They must be quite a family, taking on a project like that. Do they have any outside help?"

"At first it was just them, but now they have regular volunteers. And some who just pitch in when they can." Max drank his juice. "I volunteered when I was here before. That's how I spent the last three months of my sabbatical, helping out at the orphanage."

Lizzie hadn't realized the extent of his commitment. She'd assumed he'd merely visited the place. "No wonder you know so much about it."

He offered more of his knowledge by saying, "Nulah didn't used to allow international adoptions. But they finally decided it was in the best interest of the children. Otherwise, finding homes for these kids would be even more difficult. There aren't enough local families who have the means to take them. The older folks are dying off, and most of the younger ones are struggling to raise their own children."

He paused to watch a pair of colorful seabirds soaring along the shore. Lizzie watched them, too, thinking how majestic they were.

Then he said, "Not all of the kids at the orphanage are up for adoption. Losa is fostering some of them, keeping them until they can return to their families. But either way, she devotes her life to the children in her care, however she can."

"She sounds like a godsend."

"She is. She spent years lobbying for the international adoption law here. Without her, it might never have happened."

Clearly, Losa had strength and fortitude, seeing things through to the end. "When we're on the mainland, I'd like to stop by a florist and get her a rose."

"You want to give her a flower that matches her name?"

"Mama always taught me that you should bring someone a gift the first time you visit." She paused to reflect. "I should bring something for the kids, too. Not just for Tokoni, but for all of them. How many are there?"

"The last time I was here, it was around thirty. It's probably still about the same."

"And what's the age range?"

"It varies, going from babies to young teens."

"That's a wide margin. I'm going to need a little time to shop for a group like that. We should leave for the mainland soon." Lizzie was anxious to get started. "We can take the next boat."

He grinned. "Then maybe we should eat a little faster."

She knew he was kidding. He'd already wolfed down most of his meal. Hers was nearly gone, too. "It's delicious." She raised her fork. "These crepes."

"This island is paradise." He stopped smiling. "If only everything on the mainland was as nice as it is here."

"Yes, if only." She'd caught glimpses of the capital city yesterday and had seen how poverty-stricken some of the areas were, the places where the kids from the orphanage had come from. And if anyone could relate to their ravaged beginnings, it was Max. He'd been born in South Dakota on one of the poorest reservations in the States, before his mother had hauled him off to an impoverished Los Angeles neighborhood.

As lonely as Lizzie's childhood had been, she'd never known the pain and fear of being poor. But that hadn't stopped her and Max from becoming friends. They'd formed a bond, regardless of how different they'd been from each other.

Trapped in emotion, she said, "Thank you."

He gave her a perplexed look. "For what?"

For everything, she thought. But she said, "For inviting me to take this trip with you."

"I'm glad you're here, too."

Their gazes met and held, but only for a moment.

Returning to their food, they fell silent, fighting the ever-present attraction neither of them wanted to feel.

Max and Lizzie got to the mainland around eleven, and he hailed a cab. Taxis weren't metered here, so they had to agree on the price of the fare before departure. Max arranged to keep the taxi at their disposal for the rest of the day. Their driver was a big, broad-shouldered twentysomething with a brilliant smile. As pleasant and accommodating as he was, he drove a bit too fast. But tons of cabbies in the States did that, too. As for the car, it was old and rickety, with seat belts that kept coming unbuckled. But it was better than no transportation at all, Max thought.

As they entered the shopping district, the car bumped and jittered along roughly paved roads. The still-smiling cabbie found a centrally located parking spot and told them he would wait there for them. To keep himself occupied, he reached for his phone. Max, of course, was consumed with technology, too. It was his world, his livelihood, his outlet. But he never buried his face in his phone when he was with Lizzie. She hated it when people ignored each other in favor of their devices, so he'd made a conscious effort not to do that to her.

Behaving like tourists, they wandered the streets, going in and out of small shops. Some of the vendors were aggressive, trying as they might to peddle their wares. But Max didn't mind. He understood that they had families to feed. He went ahead and purchased a bunch of stuff to ship back home, mostly toys and trinkets for his nieces—his foster brothers' adorable little daughters.

Lizzie wasn't faring as well. Although she'd already gotten a stack of baby goods for the infants and toddlers at the orphanage and placed them in the taxi for safekeeping, she couldn't make up her mind about the rest of the kids.

Finally she said, "Maybe I can put together a big box of art supplies that all of them can use."

"That's a great idea. Tokoni would appreciate it, too, since he loves to draw. There's an arts and crafts store around the corner. They also have a little gallery where they sell works by local artists. I always wanted to check it out."

"Then let's go." She seemed interested in the art, too. "But first I want to get what I need for the kids."

They walked to their destination. The sun was shining, glinting beautifully off her ponytailed hair. He'd teased her earlier about her looking like a socialite who was trying to go incognito. In his opinion, Lizzie wasn't the type who could downplay her breeding. She'd already spent too many years perfecting it, and by now it was ingrained into the woman she'd become.

When they came to the arts and crafts store, they went inside, and she gathered paints, brushes, crayons, markers, colored pencils, paper, blank canvases and whatever else she could find. She added crafts, too, like jewelry-making kits and model cars. The man who owned the shop was thrilled. He was a chatty old guy who introduced himself as George. Max figured it was the English translation of his birth name.

After Lizzie made her purchases, she and Max browsed the work that was for sale in the gallery section. George followed them. Hoping, no doubt, that Lizzie was an art collector.

Only it was Max who got curious about a painting. It depicted a ceremony of some sort, where a young couple was cutting pieces of each other's hair with decorative knives. In Native American and First Nations cultures, shearing one's hair was sometimes associated with death and mourning. But the people in this picture didn't appear to be grieving.

While he inspected the painting, Lizzie stood beside him. George was nearby, as well.

"What are they doing?" Max asked him.

The owner stepped forward. "Preparing for their wedding. It's an old custom, chopping a betrothed's hair. Doing this symbolizes their transitions into adulthood."

Max frowned. "I'd never do that."

"Do what? Cut your lady's hair?" By now George was gazing at Lizzie's bright red locks.

"I meant get married." Max shook his head. "And she isn't my lady. She's my friend."

"Hmm." George tapped his chin. "Is this true?" he asked Lizzie. "You're only friends with this man?"

"Yes, that's all we are," she assured him.

"It's different for me," he said. "I have a wife." He took her hand and tugged her toward the other side of the gallery. "You come, too," he told Max. "I'll show you something else."

As soon as Max spotted the painting George wanted them to see, he stopped to stare at it. The nearly life-size image depicted a wildly primitive young woman on a moonlit beach, dancing with a male partner, only he was made completely of fire. She swayed in his burning-hot arms, with her long slim body draped in a sparkling gold dress. Her flame-red hair blew across her face, shielding her mysterious features from view.

"It's called *Lady Ari*," George said.

Max sucked in his breath. "After the royal goddess of fire." He hadn't known her name until now.

"Yes," George said. "With hair like your friend's." He glanced over at Lizzie.

Max shifted his attention to her, too, but she didn't acknowledge him. She continued looking at the painting. Was she as captivated by it as he was, or was she focusing on the picture so she didn't have to return his gaze?

He couldn't be sure. But the feverish feeling *Lady Ari* gave him was too overpowering to ignore. "I'm going to buy it." Now, he thought, today.

With a sudden jolt, Lizzie jerked her head toward his. "And do what with it?"

"I'll hang it in my house." He considered where to put it. "Above the fireplace in my den."

"You already have a nice piece of artwork there."

"So I'll replace it with this one."

She fussed with her ponytail, as if she was fighting its brazen color, and he realized how uncomfortable his attraction to *Lady Ari* was making her. But he simply couldn't let the painting go.

As they both fell silent, Max noticed that George was watching the two of them, probably thinking what strange friends they were. But nonetheless, the older man was obviously pleased that he'd just made a significant sale.

"The artist would be enchanted by you," George told Lizzie. "You would be charmed by him, too. He's young and handsome." He then said to Max, "A lot like you."

Lizzie raised her eyebrows at that, and Max shrugged, as if the artist's virility was of no consequence. But it made him feel funny inside, with George making what seemed like romantic comparisons.

Still, it didn't change his interest in buying it. The need to have it was too strong. Max arranged to have the painting shipped home, as he'd done with the items he'd bought for his nieces.

After the transaction was complete, they said goodbye to George and returned to their taxi, piling the art supplies Lizzie had purchased into the trunk.

She scowled at Max and said, "I still have to get Losa a rose."

"Okay, but don't be mad about the painting."

"I'm not."

Yes, she was, he thought. She didn't like the idea of him owning a picture that could be mistaken for an untamed version of her. But he wasn't going to apologize for buying something he wanted.

"Do you know where the florist is?" she asked him.

"No." He didn't have a clue. He checked with their driver and was informed that it was close enough to walk, so they set out on foot again.

The florist offered a variety of exotic plants and blooms. Max waited patiently while Lizzie labored over what color of rose to buy.

She decided on a pale yellow, and they returned to the taxi and climbed into the car. The driver started the engine and off they went, en route to the orphanage.

After a beat of silence, she said, "I wonder who modeled for it."

For it. The painting. Obviously her mind was still on *Lady Ari*. "I assumed that the artist had created her from his imagination."

She sat stiffly in her seat, clutching the rose. "I should have asked George, but I didn't think of it then. I'd prefer that she was a real person."

"Why? Because then she would seem less like you and more like the model? Just think of how I feel, knowing the artist is a handsome guy who's supposedly a lot like me."

She narrowed her eyes at him. "It serves you right. I mean, really, what were you thinking, buying something like that?"

He defended himself. "You ought to be glad that I did."

"Oh, yeah? How do you figure?"

"Because now I can lust over the painting and forget that I ever had the hots for you."

"You wish." As they rounded a corner, he leaned into her. She shoved him aside. "And stop crowding me."

Max cursed beneath his breath. He wasn't invading her space purposely. The force of the turn had done it. He wanted to tell the driver to slow down, that this wasn't the damned Autobahn. Instead he said to Lizzie, "You're nothing like Lady Ari. It's not as if you'd ever dance that way in the moonlight."

"Gee, you think?" She waved her arms around, willy-nilly. "Me and a male heap of burning fire?"

"That was the worst sensual dance I've ever seen."

"That was the idea."

"To suck?"

The taxi came to a quick halt, stopping for a group of pedestrians. Max and Lizzie both flew forward and bumped their foreheads on the seats in front of them.

He turned to look at her, and she burst out laughing. He did, too. It was impossible to keep arguing in the midst of such absurdity.

"I'm sorry for giving you a hard time," she said. "You can buy whatever artwork you want."

"I'm sorry, too." He leaned toward her and whispered in a mock sexy voice, "I didn't mean what I said about forgetting that I have the hots for you. Even if you can't dance like her, you're still a temptress."

She accepted his flirtation for what it was. But she also pushed him away from her again, keeping him from remaining too close.

Then...*vroom*! The car sped off, taking them to the grassy outskirts of town, where the orphanage was.

Three

The orphanage was in a renovated old church, large enough to accommodate its residents and perched on a pretty piece of land with a cluster of coconut trees.

A short stout lady greeted them on the porch. With plainly styled gray hair and eyes that crinkled beneath wire-rimmed glasses, she appeared to be around seventy. Max introduced her as Losa.

After they shook hands, Lizzie extended the rose. "This is for you."

"Thank you. It's lovely." The older woman accepted it with a gracious smile. Although she gazed at Lizzie's fiery red hair, she didn't comment on it.

Thankfully, that made the painting Max had bought seem less important. For now, anyway. No doubt *Lady Ari* would keep creeping back into

Lizzie's mind, along with Max's sexy little joke about Lizzie tempting him.

Clearing her wayward thoughts, she said, "I also brought gifts for the kids." She gestured to the boxes Max had placed beside the door. "I got blankets and bottles for the babies and art supplies for the rest of them."

"That's wonderful." Once again, Losa thanked her. "You seem like a nice girl."

"She is," Max said. "We've known each other since high school. We've been proper friends a long time."

Proper friends? Was that his way of making sure that Losa didn't mistake them as lovers, the way George had done? That was fine with Lizzie. She preferred to avoid that sort of confusion.

Losa invited them into her office, a simply designed space that was as understated as she was. Max brought the boxes inside and put them next to a metal file cabinet.

Losa offered them iced tea that had been chilling in a mini fridge and slices of homemade coconut bread that were already precut and waiting to be served.

They sat across from her with their food and drink, near a window that overlooked the yard.

Lizzie noticed a fenced area with picnic benches, occupied by groups of children who appeared to be between the ages of two and five. Two colorfully dressed young women watched over them.

Losa followed her line of sight and said, "The

older children are in school and the babies are in the nursery. The others are having lunch, as you can see. Tokoni is among them. You can visit with him afterward."

Lizzie didn't ask which child was Tokoni or try to recognize him from the photo Max had shown her, at least not from this distance. She was still nervous about meeting him, especially with how much Max adored him.

"So," Losa went on to say, "you want to interview me for your charity blog?"

"Yes," Lizzie quickly replied, "I'd like to feature the orphanage. To provide whatever information you're willing to give." She removed her phone from her purse. "Also, may I get your permission to do an audio recording? It's more accurate than taking written notes."

"Certainly," Losa said. "It's good of you to help. It was kind of Max to donate to us, too. He was very generous." She sent him an appreciative smile.

Although he returned her smile, he stayed quiet, drinking his tea and allowing Lizzie to do the talking.

Once the recording app was activated, she said to Losa, "Max told me that you and your family founded this orphanage after your husband passed."

"He was a dear man." Her expression went soft. "He would be pleased by what we accomplished here."

Lizzie stole another glance at the window. "Are

those your granddaughters? The young women tending to the kids?"

"Yes. They're good girls, as devoted as I am to keeping this place going and matching our children in waiting with interested families. Tokoni is especially eager to be adopted. He chatters about it all the time."

Lizzie nodded. Max had said the same thing about him. "I'm hoping that my article will raise more than just money for your cause. That it will bring awareness to the kids themselves and how badly they need homes."

"We work with international adoption agencies that provide pictures and information of our children in waiting. You're welcome to post links to those websites."

"Absolutely." Lizzie intended to be as thorough as possible. "Will you email me that information, along with whatever else you think will be helpful?"

"Actually, I can give you a packet right now." Losa went to the file cabinet and removed a large gray envelope. She resumed her seat, slid it across the desk and said, "In the United States, intercountry adoption is governed by three sets of laws—the laws of the child's country of origin, your federal laws and the laws of the US state in which the child will be adopted."

"How long does the process typically take?"

"In some countries, it can take years. For us, it's between three and six months."

"Wow. That's fast." Lizzie leaned forward. "Are

you the only country that's been able to expedite it that way?"

"No. There are others in this region. Small independent nations, like ours, with less red tape, as one might say."

"Will you tell me about your guidelines?"

"Certainly," Losa replied. "We don't have residency requirements, meaning that the applicants don't have to live here before they adopt. But we do require that they study our culture through the online classes we designed. Prospective parents may be married or single. They need to be at least twenty-five years of age and demonstrate a sufficient income. But what we consider sufficient is reasonable. We're not seeking out the rich. Just people who will love and care for these children. Honorable people," she added. "Their character is what's most important to us."

"Did you help develop these guidelines when you lobbied for international adoption?"

"I worked closely with the authorities, giving them my input. But in some cases, the requirements are modified to accommodate a family member's request. For example, Tokoni's mother asked that he be adopted by a married couple. She didn't want him being raised by a single parent." The older woman softly added, "So I promised her that he would be matched with the type of parents she envisioned, a young romantic couple who would devote their hearts to him, as well as to each other."

Lizzie considered Tokoni's mother and how terribly she'd struggled. Apparently she wanted her son to have a warm, cozy, traditional family, which was what she'd longed to give him when she dreamed of marrying his father.

Losa said, "Most of our applicants want girls. Studies show this to be true in other countries, as well. Unfortunately, that makes it more challenging to find homes for the boys. If Tokoni were a girl, he might have been placed by now."

Lizzie's chest went heavy, tight and twisted, in a way that was beginning to hurt. "I hope the perfect parents come along for him. But you never really know what hand life will deal you. My mom died when I was ten, and my dad raised me after she was gone. But I hardly ever saw him. He was wealthy enough to hire nannies and cooks to look after me."

"I'm sorry that your father wasn't available for you," Losa said. "It shouldn't be that way."

Lizzie noticed that Max was watching her closely now. Was he surprised that she'd offered information about herself?

After a second of silence, he said, "I told Losa about my childhood last time I was here. Not all the sordid details, but enough for her to know that I came from an abusive environment."

"So much sadness." Losa sighed. "Perhaps spending a little time with Tokoni will cheer you up. He's such a vibrant boy."

Lizzie glanced out the window. By now the children had finished eating and were playing in the grass. She watched them for a while, analyzing each one. Was Tokoni the boy in the green shirt and denim shorts? He appeared to be about the right age, with a similar haircut to that of the child in Max's picture, with his bangs skimming his eyes. He was laughing and twirling in the sun, like the happy kid he was supposed to be.

"Their recess is almost over," Losa said. "And as soon as they come inside, you can meet him."

"Yes, of course." Since the interview was coming to a close, Lizzie turned off the recorder on her phone and gathered the packet she'd been given. "I'm looking forward to it."

"Splendid." Losa stood. "You can chat with him in the library. We use it as an art room, too, so that's where the supplies you brought will be kept." She said to Max, "You know where the library is, so you two go on ahead, and I'll bring Tokoni to you."

Lizzie put on a brave face, but deep down she was still concerned that Tokoni would find her lacking. That he wouldn't take to her the way he had with Max.

But it was too late to back out. She was here to support Max—and the orphaned child they'd come to see.

The library was furnished in the typical way, with tables and chairs and shelves of books, but as Lizzie and Max stepped farther into the room, she spotted a seating area in the back that she assumed was designed for guests.

Max led her toward it, and they sat on a floral-printed sofa. She folded her hands on her lap, then unfolded them, attempting to relax.

"It feels good to be back," he said, far more comfortable than she was. "I miss volunteering here."

"What kinds of things did you do?" she asked, trying to envision him in the throes of it.

"Mostly I read to the kids or told them stories. But sometimes I helped in the kitchen. I fixed the plumbing once and mopped the floors in the bathroom when one of the toilets overflowed. Tokoni got in trouble that day because he caused the problem, flushing a toy boat down there."

She bit back a laugh. Apparently sweet little Tokoni had a mischievous side. "I guess your donation didn't make you immune to the grunt work."

"I didn't think it was fair for me to pick and choose my tasks. Besides, as much as Losa appreciated the money, she understood that I needed to be useful in other ways, too."

"The kids must have gotten used to having you around."

He smiled. "Yeah, they did. That's how Tokoni and I got so close."

Just then Losa entered the library, clutching the boy's hand. He was the kid in the green shirt and denim shorts Lizzie had noticed earlier, and up close he looked just like the picture Max had shown her, with full round cheeks and expressive eyes. As soon as Tokoni saw Max, he grinned and tried to escape Losa's hold. But she wouldn't let him go, so he stood there, bouncing in place.

Max came to his feet. Lizzie followed suit, and her nerves ratcheted up a notch.

Tokoni tried to pull Losa toward Max, but the older woman wouldn't budge. "If you want to see Max, you have to be good," she warned the child. "And then I'll come back to get you."

"Okay." He promised her that he would be "very, very good." A second later, he was free and running straight to Max.

Losa left the library, and Lizzie watched as man and child came together in a joyous reunion.

"Hey, buddy," Max said, scooping him up. "It's great to see you."

"Hi, Max!" He nuzzled the big, broad shoulder he was offered, laughing as Max tickled him.

Once the kid calmed down, he gazed curiously at Lizzie. This strange woman, she thought, who was just standing there.

She tried for a smile, but feared that it might have come off as more of a grimace. He just kept staring at her, *really* staring, to the point of barely blinking. She could tell it was her hair that caught his attention. Her dang Lady Ari hair.

With Tokoni still in his arms, Max turned to face her, too. At this point, he'd become aware of how the five-year-old was reacting to her.

"Is she a goodness?" the child asked.

"You mean a *goddess*?" Max chuckled. "No. She's just a pretty lady with red hair. But sometimes I think she looks like a goddess, too. She's my friend Lizzie."

Tokoni grinned at her and said, "Hi, Izzy."

"Hello." She didn't have the heart to correct him. But Max did.

"Her name is Lizzie," he said. "With an *L*. Like Losa. Or lizard." Max stuck out his tongue at her, making a reptile face. "I always thought her name sounded a little like that."

"Gee, thanks." She made the same goofy face at him, trying to be more kidlike. But truth of the matter, he'd nicknamed her Lizard ages ago. Just as she sometimes called him Mad Max.

Tokoni giggled, enjoying their antics.

Max said to him, "So you think we're funny, do you?"

"Yep." The child's chest heaved with excitement, with more laughter. Then he said to Lizzie, "Know what? This is an orange-fan-age."

She smiled, amused by his pronunciation of it.

"Know what else?" he asked. "My real mommy is gone, but I'm going to get 'dopted by a new mommy. And a daddy, too."

Overwhelmed by how easily he'd rattled that off, she couldn't think of anything to say. She should have been prepared for a conversation like this, knowing what she knew about him, but she couldn't seem to find her voice.

But that didn't stop him from asking her, "Why are you at the orange-fan-age?"

"Because Max wanted me to meet you."

Tokoni reached out to touch her hair, locating a

strand that had come loose from her ponytail. "How come?"

"Because of how much he likes you." She released the air in her lungs, realizing that she'd been holding her breath. "And because I'm going to write a story about the orphanage and the kids who live here."

"Can I be a superhero in it?"

Oh, dear. "It's not that kind of story."

He was still touching her hair. "It could be."

No, she thought, it couldn't. She wasn't good at writing fiction. She'd always been a reality-type gal.

"Come on, buddy," Max said, redirecting Tokoni's attention. "Let's all go over here." He carried him to the sofa and plopped him down.

Lizzie joined them, with Tokoni in the middle. She fixed her hair, tucking the loose strand behind her ear.

"I made a book of the mommy and daddy who are going to 'dopt me," he said to her. "I can show it to you."

"Sure," she replied, trying to be as upbeat about it as he was.

Tokoni climbed off the sofa and dashed over to a plastic bin that had his name on it. There appeared to be personalized bins for all the children, stacked in neat rows.

He returned and resumed his spot, between her and Max. He showed her a handmade booklet, consisting of about ten pieces of white paper with staples in the center holding it together.

He narrated each picture, explaining the activity he and his future parents were engaging in. On page one, they stood in the sun. On page two, they swam in the ocean. In the next one, they were going out to dinner, where they would eat all of Tokoni's favorite foods.

Everyone had red smiles on their faces, black dots for eyes and no noses. Dad was the tallest, Mom was wearing a triangle-shaped dress and Tokoni was the only one with hair. His folks were completely bald.

Lizzie assumed it was deliberate. That Tokoni hadn't given them hair because he didn't know what color it should be. He obviously knew that he might be adopted by people who looked different from him. Blonds, maybe? Or even redheads?

She fussed with her hair, checking the piece she'd tucked behind her ear, making sure it stayed put.

"Your book is wonderful," she said. "Your drawings are special. The best I've ever seen." She didn't know much about kids' art, but his work seemed highly developed to her, with how carefully thought out it was.

He flashed a proud smile and crawled onto her lap. She went warm and gooey inside. This child was doing things to her that she'd never felt before.

He said, "You can color inside my book if you want to."

Heavens, no, she thought. As flattered as she was by his generous offer, she couldn't handle the pressure that would cause. "That's very nice of you, but I don't think I should."

He persisted. "It's okay if you don't color very good. I'll still let you."

Her skills weren't the problem. "I just don't—"

Max bumped her shoulder, encouraging her to do it. Damn. Now how was she supposed to refuse?

"All right," she relented, her stomach erupting into butterflies. "But I'm going to sit at one of the tables." Where she could concentrate. "And I'll need some crayons." She didn't mention that she'd brought new art supplies for Tokoni and his peers, because it was up to Losa to distribute those.

After Tokoni got the crayons, he scooted next to her at the table, directly at her elbow and making it difficult for her to work. But she didn't tell him to move over. He was so darned excited to have her do this, almost as if she really was a goddess.

Max joined them, only he didn't have to draw. He got to kick back and watch. Lizzie wished she hadn't gotten roped into this. What if she ruined the boy's book? What if he didn't like what she did to it?

She opened the first page: the depiction of Tokoni and his family on a sunny day. She used an orange crayon and added more rays to the giant sun, giving it an extra pop of color. That seemed safe enough.

Tokoni grinned. What Max had told her about the boy was true. He smiled all the time.

"Do something else," he told her.

She put grass beneath the people's feet and glanced across the table at Max. He shot her a playful wink, and her pulse beat a bit faster.

Returning to the picture, Lizzie drew multicolored flowers sprouting up from the grass. "How's this?" she asked Tokoni.

"That's nice." He turned the page for her. "Do this one."

It was the ocean scene. She embellished it with bigger waves and a school of fish. She added sand and seashells, too.

Tokoni wiggled in his seat and went to the next page, where the family was going out to dinner. He said, "Make the mommy look more like a girl."

Lizzie contemplated the request. She certainly wasn't going to give the female a bust or hips or anything like that. So she detailed the mommy's dress, making it more decorative. She also gave her jewelry, a gold necklace and dangling earrings.

"That looks pretty," Tokoni said.

"Thank you." She drew high heels onto the mommy's feet.

But the poor woman looked incomplete, all dressed up with her bald head, so Lizzie included a hat with a flower poking out of it.

"Put stuff on her mouth," Tokoni said.

"Lipstick?"

He nodded.

She reached for a pink crayon. "How about this?"

"Okay." He moved even closer, eager to see the transformation.

She reshaped the mommy's lips, making them fuller but still retaining her smile.

"I think the mom needs some hair coming out

from under her hat," Max said. "The dad could use some, too. Unless he's the shaved-head type."

Seriously? Lizzie could have kicked him. With all the months he'd spent here, getting close to Tokoni, he should have known what the hairless parents were about. But sometimes men could be downright clueless, even the sensitive ones like Max.

And now poor little Tokoni was mulling over the situation, looking perplexed. "What color?" he asked Max.

Realization dawned in Max's eyes, and Lizzie squinted at him, wishing he hadn't opened this can of worms.

After a beat of outward concern, Max said, "Any color." He quickly added, "Blue, green, purple."

Tokoni laughed. "That's silly."

Max laughed, too, recovering from his blunder. "Not as silly as you think. There are people where I live who dye their hair those colors."

"You should do yours," the boy said to him.

Max ran his fingers through the blackness of his hair. "Maybe I will."

Tokoni laughed again. Then he said to Lizzie, "But not you."

She tapped the tip of his nose. As cute as he was, she couldn't seem to help herself. "You don't want me to dye my hair a funny color?"

"No. I want it to stay red."

The hair discussion ended and the mommy and daddy in Tokoni's booklet remained bald.

A short while later, Losa returned. Tokoni didn't

want to go with her, but he didn't have a choice. It was naptime. All the younger kids had to nap in the middle of the day. Or at least rest their eyes and stay quiet.

"Will you and Max come back tomorrow?" he asked Lizzie.

"Yes, absolutely," she replied. "Maybe we can volunteer for the rest of the week and see you every day, if that's all right with Losa."

The older woman readily agreed, and Lizzie's heart twirled. She wanted to spend as much time with Tokoni as she could before their trip was over. She was certain that Max did, too. He seemed pleased with her suggestion. But he'd already told her that he missed volunteering there.

"See you soon, buddy." Max got on bended knee to say goodbye to the boy, and they hugged.

Lizzie was next. Tokoni held her so warmly, so affectionately, she nearly cried. This child needed a family, and she was going to do everything within her power to help him get one.

Four

While dusk approached the sky, Lizzie and Max walked along the beach at their resort. Collecting her thoughts, she stopped to gaze at the horizon.

Reflecting on the day's events, she said what was on her mind, what she'd been consumed with since they left the orphanage. "I want to help Tokoni get adopted."

An ocean breeze stirred Max's shirt, pulling the fabric closer to his body. "You're already going to try to do that with your blog article."

"Yes, but I want to do more than just write an article that *might* help. I want to actually—" she stalled, trying to make sense of what it was she thought she was capable of "—find the perfect parents for him."

"How?" he asked. "How would you even begin to go about doing something like that?"

"I don't know." All she'd ever done was raise money for children's charities. She'd never set out to find an orphaned kid a home. "But with all my resources, with all the people I know, there has to be a way to make it happen."

He looked into her eyes, almost as if he was peering into the anxious window of her soul. "You're really serious about this."

"Yes, I am." She couldn't help how eager she was, how attached she'd already become to Tokoni. "You were right about how special he is. And I want to make a difference in his life."

His gaze continued to bore into hers. Did he think that she was getting in over her head?

Then he smiled and said, "I'll help you, Lizzie. We can do this. Both of us together. We can find him a home."

Her pulse jumped, her mind raced. Suddenly the beach seemed to be spinning, moving at a dizzying pace.

She pushed her toes into the sand, steadying herself. "Thank you, Max." He was the one true constant in her life. The person she relied on most, and if he was onboard, her quest seemed even more possible.

He kept smiling. "I loved watching you with him today. You were amazing the way you interacted with him."

She breathed in his praise. "I can't wait to see him again. But at least we've got the rest of the week."

Max's smile fell. "I can't believe how I screwed

up, saying what I did about his drawings. I should have been aware of the hair thing before now."

"It's all right. When he gets adopted by his new mommy and daddy, he can add their hair and anything else that will identify them to him."

"He was certainly fascinated with your hair. But I figured he would be."

"That made me uncomfortable at first."

"I know. I could tell." His voice went a little rough. "It sure looks wild now."

"It's just the wind." She tried to sound casual. But it wasn't easy. Before they'd ventured out to the beach this evening, she'd removed her ponytail, and now her hair was long and loose and blowing past her shoulders, probably a lot like Lady Ari's in the painting he'd bought.

Before the moment turned unbearably awkward, she redirected his focus and hurriedly said, "We're going to have to talk to Losa about our plan, since she's the one who will be approving Tokoni's prospective parents."

"In a way, we will be, too, with the way we'll be searching for them." He stooped to pick up a shell at his feet and study its corkscrew shape. He returned it to the beach and asked, "Are we really going to know, Lizzie?"

"Who's right for him? I think we will. Besides, we have the guidelines his mother set."

A hard and fast frown appeared on his face, grooving lines into his forehead. "A young romantic couple, devoted as deeply to each other as they'll be to him? That's out of our league."

A heap of concern came over her. "You're starting to sound as if you don't want to do this. Are you having second thoughts?"

"No. But I don't want to choose the wrong people. Or send the wrong applicants to Losa or whatever."

"I agree, completely. We're not going to run right out and grab the first wannabe parents who come along. Besides, we haven't even figured out the best way to approach this yet."

"You're right. Once we research the possibilities and explore our options, I won't be as worried about it."

"Whoever his parents are going to be, they need to encourage his artwork. I think he's going to excel at art. His cognitive skills blow me away, too, with the way he analyzes everything. I doubt many five-year-olds are as advanced as he is."

Max grinned. "That's exactly how I felt when I first met him. And with as happy as he is all the time, he makes everybody around him smile."

She laughed. "Gosh, do you think we're biased?"

He laughed, too. "With the way we're both singing his praises, you'd think he was our kid." His mood sobered, his handsome features going still. "But he's not."

"No, he definitely isn't." She couldn't get over the loss of her own mother, let alone become one herself. "But that isn't something we need to think about. No one is going to suggest that we adopt him."

"We couldn't even if we wanted to."

"No, we couldn't." They weren't married or in love or anything even remotely close to what Tokoni's mother had requested. "Not that you wouldn't make a great dad. It's being a husband that you would fail miserably at."

"You've got me there." He shrugged, reaffirming what they both already knew. "I definitely couldn't handle that, any more than you could cope with being a wife."

"That's for sure. I've never even dated anyone for more than three months, which is weird, when you think that someone could actually adopt Tokoni within three to six months." She added, "But that should help our cause with a couple who's eager and ready to adopt."

"You're right, Lizard." He turned playful, kicking a bit of sand at her ankles. "It should."

She kicked a bigger pile at him, some of the grains making it all the way to his knees. "Don't mess with me, Mad Max."

"Ooh, check you out," he teased her. "I should dunk your ass in the water for that."

She shot a glance at the ocean. Dusk was still closing in, painting the sky in mesmerizing hues. Bracing to get wet, to splash and frolic, she said, "If you do, I'm taking you down with me."

Yet when she turned back to gauge his reaction, a look of common sense had come into his eyes. He'd obviously thought better of it. Then again, why wouldn't he?

The only way for him to dunk her in the water would be to pick her up and carry her there, and that wouldn't be a good idea, not with how intimate it could get. Goofing around was one thing; creating intimacy was quite another.

Foolish as it was, she actually wished that he would lift her into his arms and haul her off to the sea. But that was just a side effect of the yearnings between them. Lizzie knew better than to want what she shouldn't have or push the boundaries of their attraction. But darned if he didn't affect her in ways she was struggling to control.

"You know what I could use about now?" He gestured in the direction of the resort's palm-thatch-roofed restaurant. "A pineapple smoothie at the bar. Do you want to join me?"

"They serve smoothies?"

He nodded. "Along with the usual spirits. But I'd rather skip the alcohol and have a smoothie."

"Then I'll have one, too." A sweet, frothy concoction that would go down easy—and help her forget about the troubling urges he incited.

The bar was dimly lit, with a tiki décor and a spectacular view of the ocean. Music played from an old-fashioned jukebox. Pop tunes, mostly, from eras gone by.

Max drank his smoothie in suffering silence. Being sexually attracted to his best friend was a hell of a burden to bear. But at least the feelings were mutual and Lizzie was suffering right along with him.

They'd been dealing with this for years, so tonight was just more of the same—except for their pledge to find a family for Tokoni.

"Did you really mean what you said about me making a great dad?" he asked, breaking the silence with an emotional bang.

"Yes, I meant it." She stirred her smoothie with her straw. "You've always had a natural way with kids. It's a wonderful part of who you are."

"Thanks, but I've never actually considered being a father, not with the loner life I've chosen to lead. Now it seems sort of sad to think that I might never have kids." He glanced out the window at the darkness enveloping the sea. "But I guess being around Tokoni is making me feel that way."

"You could still have children someday if you wanted to."

"Yeah, right." He struggled to fathom the idea. "And who am I supposed to have these kids with?"

"You could adopt and become a single dad."

"I don't think that's very common."

"No, but it's still possible in this day and age, depending on the circumstances. Now, me…" She heaved a heavy sigh. "I'm not cut out to be a mom."

"You could've fooled me, with how beautifully you engaged with Tokoni."

"I'd be scared to death to be responsible for a child, to give him everything he needs."

He knew that she was referring to emotional needs. "You've always been there for me when I needed someone to lean on."

"I'm your friend. That isn't the same as being someone's mom."

"No, but it's still a testament to who you are. And so is your commitment to Tokoni. Truthfully, I'm starting to think you'd make an amazing mom."

"I don't know about that." She shook her head. Her hair was still windblown from the beach, as gorgeous as ever. "But thank you for saying it."

"I meant it." He honestly did. "Of course all that really matters is for Tokoni to have the parents he longs for."

"Does he know that you were once eligible for adoption?"

"No. I've never told him anything about my childhood, and thankfully he's never asked. But I was just one of many. About half the kids who enter the foster care system are eligible for adoption. Even now there are over a hundred thousand children in waiting." Max knew the numbers well. He helped run a foster children's charity that he and his brothers had founded. "Typically, foster kids are adopted by their foster parents. Or by extended family. That's the most common scenario."

She sighed. "Not for you, it wasn't."

Max nodded. His extended family had been as bad as his mother. He'd even had a bitter old grandmother back on the reservation who used to call him an *iyeska*, a breed, because she believed that he was half white, spawned by one of the Anglo men Mom used to mess around with in the border towns. Mom, however, had insisted that he was a full-blood and his daddy was a res boy. Till this day, he didn't have a clue who'd fathered him. He'd never been accepted by his grandmother, either. She'd died a long time ago.

"I never wanted to be adopted, anyway," he said.

"Not even by any of your foster parents?"

"I preferred being left alone. Besides, I got shifted around so much in the beginning I never got close to any of them. Of course when I met Jake and Garrett, things got better." Two other misplaced foster boys, he thought, who'd become his brothers. "But you already know that story."

"Yes. I do." She relayed the tale. "Jake was leery of you at first because he thought you were a dork. Garrett, however, was your protector from the start and would fight off the kids who bullied you."

"Garrett saved my hide more times than I can count. But Jake came around, too, and accepted me."

"It's strange how I don't know them very well, even after all these years. I see them at fund-raisers and whatnot, but that's as far as it goes."

Max had never considered how superficial her relationship with his foster brothers was. Was that his fault for not bringing her together with them in a closer way? Probably, he thought. But he wasn't good at family-type ties. Sometimes he even shielded himself from his brothers. He'd cut everyone off during his sabbatical, including Lizzie.

"I missed you," he said, blurting out his feelings.

She blinked at him. "What are you talking about?"

"When I was gone. When I was traveling." Was

that a stupid thing for him to admit? Or even think about now that she was here with him?

She gazed at him from across their rugged wood table. "I missed you, too. It was a long time for us to be apart."

"I needed to get away. It was just something I had to do."

"It's okay. I didn't feel abandoned by you. I knew you were coming back. And look how it turned out. You found Tokoni on that trip."

"And now we're going to work toward finding him the parents he dreams about," he said, confirming their plans once again.

And hoping they could actually make them come true.

Lizzie and Max's week of volunteering at the orphanage went well. And now, on their very last day, Lizzie was making banana pudding, Tokoni's favorite dessert, for all the children to enjoy. She was using a recipe that Losa's oldest daughter, Fai, had given her. Fai was the primary cook at the orphanage, but she was staying out of the kitchen today.

Nonetheless, Lizzie wasn't doing this alone. Max and Tokoni were helping her. She'd put Tokoni on banana duty, sitting him at a table where he could peel the 'nanas, as he called them. Max was seated across from him, slicing the fruit and dumping the pieces into a bowl. Later, they would be layered into casserole dishes.

"Come on, buddy." Max spoke gently but firmly

to the boy. "If you keep doing that, there won't be anything left for me to cut."

Tokoni had already squished the banana that was in his hand. He could be quite the mischief maker when he wanted to be. Lizzie laughed as Tokoni stuffed a small glob of it into his mouth and ate it.

"Don't encourage him," Max said to her.

"Sorry. But after my mom was gone, my revolving-door nannies would bring me into the kitchen so I could observe our chefs preparing their masterpieces, except I always had to sit quietly and observe, like the proper little lady that I was." She glanced at the mess Tokoni was making. "It's nice to see a kid goofing around."

"Okay." Max smiled at her. "Then you're forgiven. You, too," he said to Tokoni. "Only maybe I better get you cleaned up a bit." Max got up and wet a towel at the sink. He returned and wiped the child's face and hands.

Afterward, Tokoni asked Lizzie, "What are 'volving-door nannies?"

Oh, goodness. She should have known better than to say that. Tokoni was a highly observant boy, picking up on just about everything around him.

"Nannies look after children, sort of like teachers and nurses. I had lots of them when I was young, so that's why I said revolving door. They never stayed at my house for very long."

"How come?"

"Because it wasn't a very fun place to work."

"How come?" he asked again. He was prone to

do that, to keep asking until he got an answer that satisfied him.

Lizzie glanced at Max. He was silent, watching her, obviously waiting to see how she was going to handle this.

"I didn't smile and laugh all the time, like you do," she told Tokoni.

"Were you sad?"

She wasn't going to lie. "Sometimes, yes."

"'Cause your mommy was gone?"

Well, there you go. He'd picked up on that, too. "Yes."

"Is she gone like my mommy is gone? Is she in heaven?"

Lizzie turned down the heat on the mixture that she'd been stirring, letting it simmer on its own. Leaning against the counter, she said, "Yes, that's exactly where my mommy is." Only she couldn't tell him that her troubled Southern belle mother had chosen to be there.

"I don't 'member my mommy, but Mrs. Losa says that she loved me."

Lizzie fought back a glaze of tears. No way was she going to cry in front of this sweet, comforting child. "Losa told us about your mommy, too."

"I don't have any pictures of her. Do you have pictures of your mommy?"

"Yes, they're in an album at my house." Photos that Lizzie rarely looked at anymore.

He tilted his head. "Was her hair like yours?"

"No, it was blond. Yellow," she clarified, "and

always all done up." She made an upswept motion. "She wore fancy clothes and lots of jewels, too." Lizzie had inherited her mother's diamonds and pearls. She lowered her hands. "My dad is a ginger, though, like me."

"Ginger?"

"That's what some people call redheads."

Tokoni peeled another banana, neatly this time. "Is Ginger the name of a goodness? I mean a goddess?" he corrected himself, peering at her with his big brown eyes.

Max was looking at her, too. He stood beside the table with the damp towel still in his hands.

She replied, "No. Ginger isn't a goddess. In some places, it's been used to make fun of redheads. But now lots of redheads are claiming it as their own and making it a good thing. Ginger is a spice that people cook with that gives food a reddish tinge. There was also a character on an old TV show named Ginger who had red hair. I've heard that it might have come from her, too, but I'm not sure."

"What was she like?" Tokoni asked.

"She was a movie star who got stranded on an island with some other people when the boat they were on was caught in a storm. It sounds serious, but it was a funny show."

Max was smiling now. "The island wasn't like this one. It was uncharted, meaning that no one knew where it was. They built their own huts and ate lots of coconuts."

"We eat lots of coconuts here!" Tokoni got excited.

Lizzie replied, "Yes, you most certainly do." Losa's grandsons tended to the trees. They had a vegetable garden on the property, too. "But if we don't get back to the pudding we're making, it's never going to get done."

"We better hurry," the boy said to Max.

"You bet." Max returned to his seat and pretended to cut the bananas really fast.

Tokoni exaggerated peeling them, too. Then he said, "I wish this wasn't your last day."

"I know. Me, too." Max cleared his throat. "But we'll come back and see you again." He looked at Lizzie. "Won't we?"

"Yes, we definitely will." They couldn't tell Tokoni that they were going to try to find a family for him in the States. They discussed it with Losa, of course, and she was open to the idea, as long as they understood the challenges associated with it. Lizzie wasn't expecting it to be easy. But she wanted to stay as positive as she could.

Immersing herself in her task, she turned away to beat egg yolks in a bowl and add them to the mixture she was cooking. Lots of pudding for lots of kids, she thought. She couldn't imagine cooking regularly for this crowd.

"Is your mommy in heaven, too?" Tokoni asked Max suddenly.

Lizzie spun around. So far, Max had gotten away with not having to tell Tokoni about his childhood. But now he'd been put on the spot. He certainly couldn't claim that his mean-spirited mother had bypassed heaven and gone straight to hell, even if that was the answer buried deep in his eyes.

"Yes, she's gone," he said.

"Do you any have pictures of her?"

"No." He quickly added, "But I have pictures of my brothers on my phone that I can show you. I have two brothers, and they both have kids. Jake's daughter is a baby, and Garrett is adopting a little girl who belongs to his fiancée, the woman he's going to marry."

"He's 'dopting a kid?" Tokoni wiggled in his chair, gratification written all over his face. "He must be a nice guy."

"He is. Very nice. Both of my brothers are. After my mom went away, I became a foster kid. I lived in other people's homes because I didn't have anywhere else to go. Sort of like the foster children who stay here."

Tokoni nodded in understanding.

Max continued, "And that's where I met my brothers. Jake lost his parents, too, and Garrett's mommy was too sick to take care of him. But she got better. Or as well as she could."

"Better enough for him to go back to her?"

"Yes."

"Did you or your other brother ever get 'dopted?"

"No, neither of us ever did."

Max exchanged a glance with Lizzie, and she thought about how he hadn't wanted to be adopted. Of course he wasn't about to reveal that to Tokoni.

"I'm going to get 'dopted," the boy said. "I know I will."

Lizzie smiled, encouraging his dream. "I know you will, too."

Tokoni beamed, and her heart swelled, especially when he came over to her and wrapped his arms around her middle, giving her an impromptu hug. She reached down and smoothed his bangs, moving them out of his eyes, and for one crazy, beautiful moment, she believed what Max had said about her was true: that she would make an amazing mom.

But she shook off the feeling. This wasn't about her maternal stirrings, no matter how incredible they seemed. This was about uncovering the parents Tokoni was meant to have.

Five

Max and Lizzie were home, seated across from each other at a hectic little sandwich shop. They'd both gotten the same thing: turkey and Swiss clubs, side salads and lemonade. She looked tired, he thought. For the time being, he was exhausted, too.

They'd been back in LA for a month, working nonstop on their goal of finding Tokoni a family, using every resource they could think of. She'd written and posted her original blog article, along with a special feature on Tokoni. She'd also crafted tons of articles as a guest blogger on international adoption sites. Max had created a slew of social media accounts dedicated to their cause, and today, before stopping for this quickie lunch, they'd met with an adoption attorney to give him a packet about the orphanage in case he had any clients who might be interested in a boy Tokoni's age. This wasn't the first attorney they'd spoken to nor would it be their last. They had a checklist a mile long.

"You seem discouraged," Lizzie said. "But we knew this wasn't going to be easy."

"I'm not discouraged. I'm just—" he searched his befuddled mind for the right word and came up with "—worried."

She shifted in her chair. "About what?"

"The way I feel. How this is affecting me. How it's draining you. How it's making zombies out of us."

She furrowed her brow. "I'm doing fine."

"Are you? Are you really?" The late-afternoon light from a nearby window showcased the pale lavender circles beneath her eyes. "I think it's taking an emotional toll on you."

"So what are you saying? That you want us to slow down?" She frowned directly at him. "Or quit and leave that poor little boy in the orphanage? I can't do that. It'll break my heart not to try to give him the family he deserves."

"I'm not suggesting that we stop or slow down. I'm—" Once again, he faltered, struggling to say what he meant.

"You're what?" She picked at a corner of her sandwich, eating it like a bird.

"I've been thinking a lot about us lately. You and me. And how we would be better parents for Tokoni than these strangers we keep searching for. So far, no one else has even taken an interest in him. And even if someone does, are they going to care about him as much as we do?" *There.* He'd said it. He'd admitted the true reason for his exhaustion. Max wasn't physically tired. It was his heart that was working overtime.

"Oh, my God." She released a jittery breath. "Do you hear what you're saying?"

"That I wish we could adopt him? Yes, I'm hearing it." From his own parched lips. He grabbed his drink and took a swig.

"It's impossible. You know Losa would never let us adopt him. We don't meet his mother's requirements. We aren't who she envisioned for him."

"I know, but it shouldn't matter that we're single. We'd still make the best parents he could ever have."

She picked at her food again. "Do you really believe that? Even about me? Am I really the best mom he could have?"

"Yes, you are. Look what you're going through to find him a family. There isn't another woman on earth who's fighting for his happiness the way you are." Max still hadn't taken a bite of his sandwich yet. But he was watching Lizzie, sweet, delicate, ladylike Lizzie, dissect hers.

"On our last day at the orphanage, when we were making the pudding, I was starting to feel like a mom." She tore at a slice of tomato. "But I knew better than to focus on it."

"It isn't fair that his mother set such strict requirements. Every other kid in that place is allowed to be adopted by a single parent. And in our case, Tokoni would be getting two single parents, a mom and a dad, who would raise him with as much love and care as he needs."

"Except that we would be parenting him from separate households," she pointed out.

"There's nothing wrong with that. Our friendship is stronger than most marriages, anyway."

"I agree, completely. But Losa is bound by their laws to follow his mother's instructions. She couldn't let us adopt him, even if she wanted to." Lizzie's voice rattled. "She already told us how imperative it was for him to be adopted by a married couple."

Max made a frustrated rebuttal. "Do you know how many people get divorced and fight over their kids or use them as pawns? What if that happens with Tokoni's future parents? What if their relationship turns bitter and he gets caught in the cross fire?"

"That's out of our control. Or Losa's or anyone's. All any of us can do is try to find him the parents his mother wanted him to have and pray for the best. I don't want to think the worst. It makes me too sad." She tore at her sandwich again, looking as if she might cry. "I need to believe that everything will work out."

"I'm sorry. I shouldn't have put such a negative spin on it. We'll just keep going, moving forward to find him a family." Even if it hurt, he thought. Even if he was convinced that he and Lizzie were the parents Tokoni needed. He went quiet for a moment, collecting his thoughts. "Speaking of adoption, Garrett called me this morning and said that Ivy's adoption was finalized today." Ivy was the toddler who belonged to Garrett's fiancée. The child he'd told Tokoni about. "He's officially her father now."

"Oh, that's wonderful. I'm happy for him. But do you think that's part of the reason you've been hit so hard about not being able to adopt Tokoni?"

"I don't know. Maybe." He hated to think that he was comparing his life to his brother's. "Garrett and Meagan are having a party to celebrate. A big bash they're planning for the Saturday after next. Do you want to come with me?"

"Yes. I'd love to go. I've never even met little Ivy."

"Then here's your chance."

"I haven't met Meagan yet, either."

Damn, he thought. He should have introduced her to Garrett's fiancée by now. But at least he was making up for lost time. "I think you'll like her."

"I can't help being curious about her, especially with her shaky past and how she stole from Garrett. And from you and Jake, too," she quickly added.

Max nodded. Meagan had embezzled from the three of them when she worked for their accountant. Her former boyfriend had talked her into committing the crime and then ditched her after she'd gotten caught. Meagan didn't even know she was pregnant until after she went to prison. "It's awful to think that she gave birth while she was incarcerated and that the father wanted nothing to do with her or Ivy."

Lizzie blew out a sigh. "It's sort of like what Tokoni's dad did."

"Only he can't try to come back into the picture."

According to the adoption laws in Nulah, he'd relinquished his parental rights when he abandoned the boy and his mother. Even his name had been removed from the birth certificate. "Ivy's dad tried to make a claim on her."

"He did? When?"

"Soon after Garrett and Meagan got together. But he wasn't interested in his daughter. It was money he was after."

Lizzie made a tight face. "What a jerk."

"Totally. But you know what? Garrett paid him off, anyway. He just wanted to get rid of the guy so he could adopt Ivy."

"And now Garrett's her new daddy." She softened her expression. "I'm looking forward to the party. Thanks for inviting me to go with you."

"It's going to be a princess theme. Ivy was named after a princess in a children's book."

"Oh, that's cute."

"And just think, a princess theme is right up your alley, with you being a royal goddess and all."

She tossed a crumb of bread at him. "Smart aleck."

He smiled, trying to stay as upbeat as he possibly could. But that didn't change how troubled he felt inside or how much he wished that Tokoni could become their son.

The party was being held in one of the ballrooms at the luxurious beachfront hotel and resort Garrett owned. Lizzie was running a bit late, so she'd told

Max that she would meet him there, and by the time she arrived, the festivities were well underway.

Everyone had the option of donning a complimentary crown. A table at the entrance of the ballroom was filled with them, in all sorts of shapes, colors and sizes. Lizzie chose a tiara decorated with green gems because it complemented her emerald gown. The attire was formal. Costumes were encouraged, too. Girls posing as Cinderella, Snow White and the Little Mermaid ran amok. Prince Charming and knights in shining armor were favorites among the boys.

Games, party favors, face painting, lessons on how to be a prince or a princess. You name it, this party had it. There was a magnificently crafted wooden castle/playhouse for the kids, which was also big enough for the adults. Even the food appeared to be fit for royalty, with a spectacular buffet.

Lizzie scanned the crowd for Max. She found him near the castle, holding a toy scepter. He wore a black velvet tuxedo with a tailcoat, and his big, bold medieval-style crown sat high atop his head, making a strong statement.

As she approached him, she noticed that he'd forgone the customary shirt and tie. Instead, he'd paired his tux with a Princess Leia T-shirt. Lizzie smiled to herself. Max was and always would be a *Star Wars* nerd.

"Look at you," she said.

"And you." He waved his scepter at her. "Your dress is hot."

"This old thing." She laughed. Along with the long silk gown, she'd draped herself in diamonds. "I see that you found a way to sneak in your favorite princess." She poked a finger at his T-shirt. "That was clever."

"I figured it would work. This is quite the kiddy soiree, isn't it?"

"I'll say. Where's the newly adopted girl?"

"In there." He motioned to the castle.

"Are you on guard duty?" A wonderfully offbeat king, she thought, behaving like a knight.

"For now I am. I told her parents that I would hold down the fort so they could grab a bite to eat. They'll be back from the buffet soon. You should have seen Ivy when she was first announced to her guests, under her new last name. We stood in a receiving line so she could greet us."

"I'm sorry I missed that. I can't wait to meet her."

"Hold on and I'll get her for you now." Max put the scepter on a gilded ledge of the castle exterior and went inside.

He returned with a dark-haired toddler dressed in a puffy pink dress, rife with taffeta and lace. Her face was painted with glitter, and multicolored gems embellished her sparkling gold tiara.

Max scooped up her up and said, "This is Ivy Ann Snow, the belle of the ball."

Ivy gazed at Lizzie and said, "Garry do this."

Garry, she assumed, was Garrett. And "this" was most likely a reference to the party, unless it meant the adoption.

Either way, Lizzie told her, "You look beautiful, like a princess should."

The child said, "Tank you," for "*Thank* you."

Lizzie smiled. Apparently Ivy had a bit of trouble with her pronunciation. But Tokoni mispronounced some of his words, too. "I know a five-year-old boy who would have liked to be here. But he lives too far away."

"What's him name?"

"Tokoni."

"Where him live?"

"In an island country called Nulah," Lizzie replied. Ever since Max had lamented that they should be the ones to adopt him, making her long for the impossible, she missed Tokoni even more.

"Do Maddy know him?"

Maddy? It took Lizzie a second to realize that Ivy was taking about Max. "Yes, he knows him."

"Maddy my uncle."

"Your favorite uncle," he said, tickling Ivy and making her laugh.

A few giggles later, she tried to wiggle out of his arms, her attention span waning. "I go now."

"Okay, Princess." He put her down, and she dashed off, back into the castle to play with her friends. Or her subjects. Or whoever she was holding court with.

"I didn't know she called you Maddy," Lizzie said.

"When I first met her, I told her my name was Mad Max, and she turned it into Maddy."

"I like it. Maybe I'll start calling you that, too, since I started the Mad Max handle to begin with."

"Go ahead, pretty Lizard. I don't mind." He reached out to touch one of her diamond drop earrings. "Are these new?"

"No, they're from my mother's collection." She went a little breathless, having him standing so close to her. "Vintage Harry Winston."

"And this?" He skimmed her necklace. "Was it your mom's, too?"

She nodded. "Yes, except it's early Cartier." She lifted her wrist to showcase her bracelet. "And here we have Tiffany and Company." Normally she kept her mother's jewelry in a safe-deposit box at the bank. "I got into the vault, so to speak."

"What made you decide to do that?"

"They remind me of when I was a little girl, so wearing them to a child's fancy party felt right somehow." She tempered her emotions, trying to keep her voice from cracking. "Mama used to let me play with her jewelry when I was young. She would dress me up and stand me in front of the mirror, giving me the history of each piece."

"I'll bet your mother would have loved this party."

"Yes, I'm sure she would have." She took a step back, away from him. But what she really wanted was to move straight into his arms and be held by him, soothing the ache of them not being able to become Tokoni's parents.

"Hey, you two," a masculine voice said from behind them.

Lizzie and Max turned simultaneously. The man who'd spoken to them was Garrett. He stood tall and trim and polished, his jet-black hair slicked straight back, his classic tuxedo sharp and crisp. He wasn't sporting a crown. But he'd probably removed it after the opening ceremony.

Next to him and holding his hand was his fiancée. Meagan was a lovely brunette with almond-shaped eyes and waist-length hair. She wore a powder-blue gown and a silver tiara.

Garrett introduced Lizzie to Meagan, and the women smiled and greeted each other.

Afterward, Lizzie said to Garrett, "Congratulations on the adoption. I met your new daughter. She's beautiful." To Meagan, she added, "She looks like you."

"Thank you." Meagan leaned toward Garrett. "She certainly adores her new daddy."

As if on cue, Ivy poked her head out of the castle, saw her parents and ran over to them. She grinned at everyone, her puffy dress askew. Then she said, "Come," to Garrett and tugged him toward the playhouse. With her other hand, she grabbed Max, pulling him in the same direction.

Meagan laughed. "Apparently the men have been summoned."

Lizzie laughed, too. "So it seems." She watched them disappear into the castle, with the toddler leading the way.

After a stretch of silence, Meagan said, "I saw you once before. It was at a fund-raiser at the park. But it was a while ago, before Garrett and I had gone public with our relationship. So no one introduced me to you. You were off in the distance, with a group of other women."

"Was Max there, too?"

"Yes. It was the first time I met him. Later that day, Garrett told me about you and how close you and Max were. I've wondered about the two of you ever since."

Lizzie's heart went bump. "What do you mean?"

"If you were more than friends—" The brunette stalled. "I hope it was all right that I just said that."

"You're not the first person who's been curious about us." And she wouldn't be the last, Lizzie thought. "It happens all the time."

"Then you must be used to it."

Was she? At the moment, she wasn't so sure.

Meagan said, "When Garrett and I first got together, we told everyone we were just friends, when we were actually having a secret affair. So I thought maybe that's what you and Max had been doing. That at some point, your friendship had turned into more. But Garrett insisted that wasn't the case. Still, I wondered how anyone, outside of you and Max, could know the absolute truth."

"The truth is that we're just friends." Friends who wanted each other, she thought. Being painfully honest, she added, "But I'm not denying that there's an attraction between us. That we..." That they what? Wished they could be lovers, but were afraid it would ruin their friendship?

"I'm sorry. I wasn't trying to pry." Meagan made a face. "Well, maybe I was. But only because of how fascinated I was by you and Max when I first saw you."

"I've been fascinated by you, too, and your history with Garrett. You've had a lot to overcome."

"That's why we kept our relationship a secret at first. I didn't want anyone to know that I was dating one of the men I embezzled from. But Garrett convinced me that we needed to come clean."

"He's a forthright guy."

"Yes, he is. I love him so much I could burst."

Lizzie couldn't relate. So far, her experience with love hurt something fierce: the loss of her mother, the pang of not being close to her father. And now she'd begun to love Tokoni, a child who wasn't even hers.

Determined to keep a rein on her emotions, she asked, "Did Garrett happen to mention the boy that Max and I are trying to find a home for?"

"Yes, he did. If there's anything I can do to help, just let me know."

"Thanks, I will." Lizzie gestured to their surroundings, her mother's Tiffany bracelet catching the light. "I told Ivy that Tokoni would have enjoyed coming to this party. It's hard not to think of him in a setting like this."

"Oh, I'm sorry that he couldn't be here." Meagan watched her with sympathy. "You must be really attached to him."

If she only knew how attached, Lizzie thought. "Max and I both are. He's a special kid."

"It's sad to think of kids living in orphanages and foster care. My brother, Tanner, raised Ivy when I was locked up, or else she would have been placed in the system. Tanner is here tonight, with his wife. My other brother and his wife and son are here, too. They flew in from Montana."

"Sounds like you have a wonderful support group."

"I couldn't have gotten through my struggles without them. Garrett's mom has been amazing, too. And of course, Garrett's brothers. Jake and Carol were here earlier with baby Nita, but they left already. Nita was getting fussy and needed to go home for her nap. Do you know Carol? Have you seen the baby?"

"I met Carol before Jake married her, when she was working for him as his personal assistant. But I don't know her very well. I haven't seen the baby yet. I sent a gift when she was born. But she must be about four or five months old by now."

"I didn't know Carol very well at first, either. But I'm becoming really close to her and the baby. Ivy adores them, too. She thinks her cousin Nita is the most wonderful being on earth."

"It's nice that you and Carol formed a bond and that your children will grow up together." Lizzie wanted Tokoni to have that type of family, too, the loving, caring kind every child should have.

"Maybe you could join us for lunch sometime."

"You and Carol?"

"Yes."

"Thank you. I'd like that." After they exchanged numbers, programming them into their phones, Lizzie asked, "Have you and Garrett set a wedding date?"

"Not yet. I want to complete my parole first. But Garrett didn't want to wait to adopt Ivy, so he started those proceedings months ago."

Lizzie smiled. "It sure seems to have worked out."

Meagan smiled, as well. "It definitely has."

Just as their conversation came to a close, Max and Garrett returned with Ivy in tow. Garrett was carrying her. He approached Meagan, and the child leaned forward to kiss her mommy.

Lizzie's heart ached from the sweet sight.

After the smooch ended, Garrett and Meagan took their leave, hauling their little princess over to the dance floor, where a kid-friendly band prepared to play Disney tunes.

In the moment that followed, Lizzie said to Max, "Meagan invited me to have lunch sometime with her and Carol."

"That's nice. I'm glad she included you in the girly stuff."

"She's easy to talk to. We discussed all sorts of things." She quickly added, "But I didn't tell her what you said about wishing that we could adopt Tokoni. There was no point in saying anything about that."

"I haven't told anyone that, either, not when there's no way to make it happen." He bumped her shoulder with his, his jacket grazing her arm. "Unless we suck it up and get married."

Her jaw nearly hit the floor. "Please tell me that you're kidding. That you didn't mean that."

"Of course I was kidding. You didn't really think…" He hesitated, frowned, blew out a choppy breath. "Besides, in order for something like that to work, we'd have to fake everyone out and pretend to be a real couple."

Lizzie's tiara was starting to feel uncomfortably heavy. "Meagan wondered if we were having a secret affair."

His voice turned grainy. "Yeah, people sometimes wonder about that. But in order for this to work, we would have to split up after the adoption with an amicable divorce. That way, we could co-parent Tokoni and still hang out as friends."

She couldn't believe what was coming out of his mouth. "Listen to yourself, Max. You're plotting the details. You're actually starting to think about it."

"I'm just thinking out loud."

"About us faking a marriage." Confused, she shook her head. "Do you know how crazy that sounds?"

"You're right." He cleared the roughness from his throat. "I shouldn't have mentioned it."

Lizzie shifted her gaze to the parents and kids and happy festivities. Everywhere she looked, she saw what she and Max were missing. But no matter how badly it hurt, entering into a phony marriage wasn't the answer.

Was it?

Six

At 1:45 a.m. Lizzie was still awake, alone in the dark, staring at the red digits on the clock.

She couldn't stop thinking about Ivy's party and the conversation she'd had with Max.

About marrying him.

Or not marrying him.

Or adopting Tokoni.

Or not adopting him.

She wasn't supposed to be letting that discussion spin around in her brain. Yet she couldn't seem to get it out of her mind.

Her only solution was to work even harder to find prospective parents for Tokoni. To sleep tonight and get up tomorrow, refreshed and ready to go. But that was easier said than done. She would probably be up for the rest of the night, fighting this battle.

And it was all Max's fault. If he hadn't tossed that fake marriage idea out there, she wouldn't be in this insomnia mess.

Just as she cursed him, her cell phone rang.

She jumped to attention. Was it Max, having the same wide-awake struggle as her? God, she hoped not. He was the last person she wanted to talk to.

She reached for the blaring device, where it sat on her nightstand. Sure enough, it was him. His name flashed on the screen, way too bright in the dark. But instead of ignoring him, like she should've, she answered the damned call.

"What do you want?" she asked.

"I knew you would be up," he replied, undaunted by her frustration. "I can't sleep, either. Can I come over?"

She switched on the lamp beside her bed and shot a pissy glance at the clock. Three minutes had passed since she last looked at it. "Do you know what time it is?"

"Yeah, it's almost two. And I'm going to lose my freaking mind if you don't let me come over."

"All right. Fine." She gave in. If she didn't, she would only lie awake, even more embattled than before. "But you better bring some donuts. I need some comfort food."

"I'll stop by a convenience store on the way over and get a package of the powdered kind, the mini ones you used to eat when we were kids. Those always made you feel better."

"Get two packages." If she was going to pig out on itty-bitty donuts, she might as well do it right.

"Sure thing. I'll see you soon."

He ended the call, leaving her staring at the phone. What had she just gotten herself into, agreeing to entertain Max in the wee hours of the morning?

She got dressed, climbing into the nearest jeans and T-shirt. She certainly wasn't going to answer the door in her short little satin chemise. Lizzie always wore fancy lingerie to bed. Her mom used to do that, too. But she shouldn't be likening herself to her mother right now. She'd already draped herself in Mama's diamonds earlier.

Hoping that a cup of tea would help soothe her nerves, she entered her bright white kitchen and filled an old-fashioned teakettle with water. She'd bought it at an antiques store, intending to use it as a flowerpot on her patio, but changed her mind and kept it on her stove top instead.

Anxious about seeing Max, she riffled through the tin container where she stored her tea bags and chose a fragrant herbal blend.

She sat at the chrome-and-glass dining table in the morning room, adjacent to the kitchen, and waited for the whistle.

Finally, when the kettle sang its song, she removed it from the flame and fixed her tea. She put an empty cup on the counter for Max, in case he wanted some, too.

He arrived with the donuts. He handed them to her, and she offered him the tea. He opted for orange juice, getting into her fridge and pouring it himself. He was attired in the same *Star Wars* T-shirt he'd worn to the party, only he was wearing it with plaid pajama bottoms instead of a velvet tuxedo.

"I can't believe you went out of the house like that," she said.

"What can I say? I'm still the same dork I always was." He grinned and toasted her with his juice.

"Stop that." It was bad enough that he was here, rumpled from bed; she didn't need him smiling like a sexy loon.

"Stop what?"

"Nothing. Never mind." She couldn't tell him how hot he looked. Better for him to assume that he looked like a dork.

He finally stopped grinning. "I can't quit thinking about us adopting Tokoni, Lizzie."

"I know. Me, too." She carried the donuts into the morning room, where she'd left her tea. She brought a stack of napkins, as well, certain she would need them.

Max followed her, and they sat across from each other. The blinds on the window that normally bathed the table in natural light were closed. Typically, Lizzie used this room for breakfast, not for middle-of-the-night snacks.

She tore into the donuts and ate the first package, right off the bat. They tasted like the processed junk they were, cheap and stale, but satisfying, too.

"Do you want one?" she asked him.

He shook his head. "Do you think we should just do it?"

"Do what? Adopt Tokoni?" She grabbed a napkin and wiped her mouth with shaky hands. "We can't."

"We could if we followed my plan."

"And get married?" Her hands shook even more. "Then divorced later? That's cheating."

"So you're suggesting that we should stay married instead? Cripes, Lizzie, that wouldn't work."

"No." Absolutely, positively no. "I'm saying that faking a marriage is cheating and that we shouldn't do it at all. It's not fair to Tokoni's mother."

"But we'd be good parents. The best we could be to her son."

"That still doesn't give us permission to bend the rules. And what about Losa? How are we supposed to convince her that our ruse is real?"

"We'll just tell her that our quest for finding Tokoni a home created feelings for each other that we never knew we had."

She opened the second package of donuts. "Feelings?"

"Yeah, you know." He made a sour face. "We'll tell Losa that we've fallen head-over-stupid-heels in love."

"Gee, what a nice, romantic way to put it. And if your sickly expression is any indication of how in love you are, this story you cooked up is never going to fly."

"Stop giving me such a hard time. You look miserable, too."

"That's because I don't want to get married."

"I don't, either. But I want to be Tokoni's father, and I want you to be his mother. And I don't know how else to make that happen."

Heaven help them, Lizzie thought. He sounded so beautifully sincere, so deep and true, that a marriage based on a lie was beginning to seem like the right thing to do. "Do you really think we could pull this off?"

"Yes, I do. But we would have to fake it with everyone, even friends and family. We couldn't let it slip that we're only doing it for Tokoni or that we plan to get divorced later."

"Won't the divorce seem suspicious, so soon after the adoption?"

"Not if we say that we misunderstood our feelings for each other and mixed it up with our love for the boy. Besides, when people see how amicable our divorce is and how easily we've remained friends, there shouldn't be any cause for concern."

She imagined having Tokoni as her forever son, of sharing him with Max, of seeing this through. "I want to be his mom as much as you want to be his dad."

He leaned forward, lifting the hind legs of his chair off the floor. "Then let's go for it."

She looked into the vastness of his eyes. By now she could barely breathe. But she agreed, anyway.

"Okay," she said. "But what's our first step?" Besides sitting here, losing the last of their sanity? Her heart was pounding so fast she feared she might topple over.

He wasn't grounded, either, not with the way he was tipping his chair. "I think we should start by talking to Losa."

"Should we go see her?"

"Truthfully, I'd rather call her with the news." He dropped his chair back onto the floor with a thud. "In fact, we can do that later today."

Lizzie wasn't ready. "I need more time than that."

"What for?"

"To work on a script for us to follow."

"Winging it would be easier for me."

"I'd prefer to research what I'm going to say." She always prepared herself for proper speeches. "I can't just spout it off the top of my head."

"And I can't refer to something you drummed up. It'll sound canned."

She blew out a sigh. Already they were having problems, and they weren't even an official couple yet.

He glanced at the darkened window. "Maybe I should do it alone. It isn't necessary for both of us to call her, and it'll probably make me more nervous to have you there, anyway, with your handy-dandy script."

Lizzie considered his point. Lying to Losa was bad enough, but doing it together might make it worse, especially if they were out of sync. "All right, but you should go home now and try to get some rest.

It won't help your cause if you're half asleep when you profess these phony feelings of ours."

"Okay, but you better not change your mind about marrying me between now and then."

"I won't." Because as afraid as she was of becoming Max's temporary wife, she was more afraid of losing the child they so desperately wanted.

Max did it. He'd talked to Losa. And now he was back at Lizzie's house, sitting on her artfully designed patio, with its built-in barbecue and portable bar, preparing to tell her how the discussion went. He glanced around and noticed that the greenery seemed far more tropical than he recalled it being in the past, as if she'd gotten inspired by their trip to Nulah and the private gardens at the resort where they'd stayed. But this wasn't the time to comment on her plants and flowers.

"I think Losa believed me," he said.

"You *think* she believed you?" Lizzie's blue eyes locked on to his. "What's that supposed to mean?"

"It means that I told her everything I was supposed to tell her, and it seems like she bought it. Of course I felt like I was going to have a panic attack when I got to the part about how we'd fallen in love during our search to find Tokoni a family. But I played up how long you and I have known each other and how close we've always been and all that. I tried to make it sound plausible." Even now his heart was roaring in his ears, the panic he'd endured still skirting through his blood. "Luckily, I didn't have to fake the part about how much we wanted Tokoni. That was easy to say."

Lizzie looked as nervous as he felt. "Is she going to let us adopt him?"

"She said that she can't make that determination until after we're married and start the process, like any other applicants would have to do. Legally, she can't promise him to us until we meet the requirements. But she did seem eager for us to come back after the wedding, so we can all meet in person again and discuss the specifics."

She appeared to relax, her shoulders not nearly as tense. "That seems like a positive sign."

"I thought so, too. I told her that we're planning on having a traditional ceremony. I didn't want her to think that we were going to elope or exclude our family and friends. To me, that didn't seem like what a happily engaged couple would do. I did stress, however, that we were eager to be together and bring Tokoni into our lives, so the wedding would be sooner than later."

"Sounds like you did a good job of presenting us as the type of parents Tokoni's mother wanted him to have."

He'd sure as hell tried. "Thanks. But now we really do need to hire a wedding planner and get this thing going."

"Maybe Garrett can recommend one of the events coordinators his hotel uses."

"I'll have to talk to him about it. But first I need to tell him and Jake the same story I told Losa." Only this time Max would be lying to his brothers, something he wasn't looking forward to.

"I need to tell my friends, too. And decide who is going to be part of my bridal party. I've been a bridesmaid before, so I have an inkling of what it entails."

Max nodded. He was also experienced in that regard. He and Garrett had shared the responsibility of being the best men in Jake's wedding.

She made a pained face. "What should I do about my dad? If we're having a traditional ceremony, should I adhere to protocol and ask him to walk me down the aisle?"

"I don't know, Lizzie. That's up to you." He couldn't make that determination for her. Nor did he want to. "Damn, there's so much to think about, so much to do. I'm already getting overwhelmed."

"Me, too." She smoothed the front of her buttondown blouse, fussing with the starched material, almost as if it were the lacy bodice of a wedding gown. "What about our living arrangements? Am I supposed to move in with you after we're married?"

"That makes the most sense. My house is bigger, and you can use one of the rooms in the guest wing, without anyone being the wiser."

"What about your maid service? Won't they notice that we're not staying together?"

"We can stage the master suite to give the impression that you're sleeping there. We can stage your room, too, so it appears as if we have a female visitor, a reclusive celebrity or someone that they're never going to see. They're not going to suspect it's you. Besides, it's a highly secure company, with housekeepers who are screened to work with wealthy clients and protect their privacy."

"If I move into your mansion, what should I do about this place?"

"You can say that you're going to rent it out for vacationers and whatnot, keeping it furnished the way it is. It would be an ideal condo for that."

"Except that I won't actually be renting it. I don't want out-of-towners staying in my home."

"That part doesn't matter. No one is going to delve that deeply into your business affairs." He considered another aspect of the plans. "If we're going to announce our engagement, then I need to hurry up and buy you a ring."

"You're right. Everyone will be asking to see it. Whenever one of my friends gets engaged, that's the first thing that comes up."

He didn't doubt it. "I'll arrange for a jeweler to bring some rings by for you to choose from. We can meet at my house, maybe later in the week."

She frowned at her left hand, where the bauble was going to go. "I'll be sure to return it to you after the divorce."

He shook his head, refusing her offer. "I don't want it back."

"But you could resell it."

"I'd rather that you kept it. You can lock it away with the jewelry your mom gave you, as a keepsake or investment or whatever."

"What about a wedding band for you?"

"I'll have the jeweler bring those, too. We can do it in one fell swoop. And hopefully with the least amount of fanfare possible." But even as he said it, he knew it wasn't going to be a casual process, not when it involved a ritual created for people who were supposed to be in love.

Although Lizzie had been to Max's house more times than she could count, she'd never expected that she would be living there. Yet that was what would be happening, soon enough.

The three-story mansion had a spiral staircase in the center of the home that curved with an air of mystery. There was also a large entryway, a woodsy den, a formal drawing room and a screening room. On the third floor was a ballroom with a wraparound balcony, designed for glamorous parties. The original owner was the head of a movie studio, way back when.

The servants' quarters were located on the first level, directly off the kitchen, but Max didn't have a live-in staff. The maid service he used kept things tidy, and when he wasn't eating out, he cooked for himself. A chef wasn't necessary.

The mansion itself probably wasn't necessary, either, Lizzie thought. But Max had bought it to console the poor battered boy he'd once been, fascinated by its rich 1930s charm.

Today she and Max occupied the den, waiting for the jeweler to arrive. While she sat on an art deco settee, he stood beside the fireplace, with the painting of Lady Ari showcased above it. She couldn't deny how nicely the artwork complemented the spot he'd chosen for it.

Was this really happening? Was she actually going to become his bride?

"I'm getting stage fright," she said.

"About picking out rings?"

"About all of it. It's weird, but I wish my mom was here to help me through it. She loved big fancy occasions."

"I'm sorry you have to face this without her."

As much as her mother's suicide hurt, Lizzie couldn't bear to hate her for it. "She would have liked you, Max. This house would have impressed her, too."

"I've been thinking that we could have the wedding here, that we could do the ceremony outside, on the lawn, and then head up to the ballroom for the reception."

She studied him: his tall, trim physique, his shiny black hair falling just shy of his shoulders. He'd never had a picnic on his lawn, let alone a wedding. He'd never used his ballroom before, either. He wasn't keen on entertaining, even if his house was wonderfully suited for it. "Are you sure you're comfortable with that?"

He shrugged. "At this point, I'd rather do it here than somewhere else. Plus it'll be easier than trying to book another venue. I'd like to set the date for two months from now. I don't want to hold up the adoption any longer than that."

"Me, neither. But we'd better be prepared for a nonstop venture, if we're going to get everything done by then."

"We'll just have to find a wedding planner who's able to speed through it."

"I'll have to put a rush on finding a dress, too." But for now she didn't have a clue what type of gown she was going to wear. "Gosh, can you imagine how strange it's going to be, with you and me, reciting vows? Talk about being nervous."

He scowled, hard and deep. "They're just words, Lizzie."

"Words about love and commitment and things that don't pertain to us."

"We're committed to Tokoni, and that's all that matters."

"You're right. I need to try to relax and go with the phony-wedding flow."

"Yes, you do. And so do I." He pasted a smile on his face. "This is supposed to be a joyous occasion. We don't want the jeweler to think there's something wrong with us."

She smiled, as well, practicing her bride-to-be expression. "This will be a good test of how we're supposed to behave."

He glanced at a cuckoo clock on the wall, a quirky old timepiece from the same era as the house. "He should be here soon."

"I wish he would hurry." She was eager to get the

ring thing over with. But thank goodness they had the luxury of the jeweler coming to them, instead of them having to go to him.

Max's gaze roamed over her. "You look pretty, by the way."

"Thank you." She was attired in a stylish tweed ensemble with her hair twisted into a neat chignon. "I tried to keep it classy."

"You always do."

"I noticed that you donned a jacket."

"Yeah." He smoothed the lapels of his sleek black sports coat. "I've got Batman on underneath, though." He opened his jacket and showed her his T-shirt.

"At least you didn't sleep in it." She gave him a double take. "Or did you?"

He laughed. "I'll never tell."

She laughed, too. "My fiancé is weird."

"Your fiancé, huh? Look who's trying out the lingo."

"After today, it will be official." Her ring would seal the deal. "So I better get used to calling you that."

"Until you have to start calling me your husband."

"Then my ex-husband." She turned serious. "Are you going to draw up a prenup for me to sign?"

"Why would I do that?"

"To protect your money. Typically, that's what rich people do when they're getting married, and you have a lot more to lose than I do."

"I don't need to protect my assets from you." He

came over and sat beside her. "You're the person I trust most in this world."

"Me, too. With you." And that was precisely why they were adopting a child together. "We're going to be awesome parents."

"The best," he agreed. "And don't worry about the wedding expenses. I'm going to pay for everything."

"You don't have to do that."

"I want to." He touched her cheek, then lifted his hand away. "But what am I going to do during the part of the ceremony where I'm supposed to kiss my bride?"

She wet her lips, a bit too quickly. "You'll have to kiss her, I guess."

"She's going to have to kiss me back, too."

Her pulse fluttered at her neck, as soft as a butterfly, as sexy as a summer breeze. "Yes, she will."

As they both fell silent, she glanced away, trapped in feelings she couldn't seem to control. She didn't want to imagine what the wedding kiss was going to be like.

Still, she wondered how it would unfold. Would he whisper something soft and soothing before he leaned into her? Would their mouths be slightly open, their eyes completely closed? Would she sigh and melt against him, like a princess being awakened by the wrong prince? Just thinking about it made her feel forbidden.

Sucking in her breath, she shifted her gaze to his. She saw that he was studying her, as if he sensed what was going on in her head. Uncomfortable in her own skin, she clasped her hands on her lap. She'd been fighting these types of urges for what seemed like forever, and now the ache had gone warm and rogue.

Brrrrinng.

The security buzzer sounded, alerting them that the jeweler had arrived at the front gate.

What timing.

Max jumped off the settee and took his phone out of his pocket. He punched out a key code and opened the gate with an app he'd designed. When he glanced up, he studied her again. "You okay, Lizzie?"

She nodded, even if she wasn't. He'd certainly recovered much easier than she had. But he wasn't the one who'd drifted into la-la land. "I'm fine."

"All right, then. I better go." He headed for the door.

"I'll stay here." And collect her composure.

While he was gone, she opened her purse and removed her compact, checking her lipstick. Nothing was out of place, of course. Max's mouth hadn't come anywhere near hers.

He returned with an older gentleman, formal in nature, who introduced himself as Timothy. The three of them gathered around a nineteenth-century mahogany card table, a focal point in the den, where Timothy could set up his portable cases. He started with the engagement rings, sweeping his hand across the impressive display once it was ready.

The diamonds were big and beautiful and dazzling. Enormous rubies, emeralds and sapphires dazzled the eye, too. But Lizzie struggled to focus. She was still stuck on that future kiss. She even bit down on her bottom lip, trying to inflict pain as a conditioned response to keep her mind off it.

Her method didn't work. Biting her lip just made her hungrier for the man she was going to marry.

"Wow. Check this out." Max lifted a ring from its slot. An oval ruby with two perfectly matched half-moon diamonds surrounding it. He said to Timothy, "This one is downright fiery." He glanced at Lizzie. "Like her hair."

His comment made her skin tingle. But she was already immersed in all kinds of heat.

Timothy glanced at her, too. Then back at Max. With a smile, he said, "Rubies are often associated with fire and passion. That particular stone is six carats and is a star ruby, a rare variety. See the starry points in the center? How they magically glide across the surface? It's an optical phenomenon known as asterism."

Lizzie finally spoke up. "It's stunning," she said about the ring. The ruby, the star, the diamonds, every glittering aspect of it.

"Try it on," Max said.

She placed it on her left hand and held it up to view. It felt right. Too right. Too beautiful. Too perfect.

Both men watched her, silent in their observations. She glanced at the painting of Lady Ari. And for a jarring instant, it almost seemed as if the goddess was watching her, too.

"That's the one, Lizzie." Max spoke up, pulling her attention back to him.

She nodded. "It is, isn't it?" She couldn't refuse the ring, no matter how much she wanted to.

Timothy suggested a petite pavé diamond band to go with it, and her bridal set was complete. Pavé was a French word, and in this context it meant that the ring was paved with diamonds, creating an unbroken circle of sparkle and light.

When Timothy presented the men's wedding bands, Max's demeanor changed. He wasn't as self-assured as when he'd been examining rings for her.

Lizzie took the liberty of choosing a design for him—a simply styled, highly masculine piece dotted with black diamonds. There was a ruby among the gems, too. Just one, she noticed, the same fiery color as hers.

When he put it on, he frowned.

"You don't like it?" she asked.

"No, I do. Very much."

Maybe too much? she wondered. Well, at least she wasn't suffering alone. They were in this torturous situation together.

And now they would both have bloodred rubies to prove it.

Seven

Max took his brothers out for a steak dinner and ordered a fancy gold bottle of Cristal. He did everything he could to make it a celebratory occasion and tell them his news, repeating the same tale he'd told Losa. At this stage of the lie, he had it memorized.

Jake accepted it easily, lifting his glass in an immediate toast. But that was Jake for you, with his half-cocked smile, fashionable wardrobe and stylishly messy hair. He'd probably never given Max's relationship with Lizzie more than a passing glance. Either that or he'd assumed the platonic part was bogus and they'd been sleeping together for years. Prior to settling down, Jake had been a playboy, dating actresses and models and whoever else caught his roving eye.

And then there was Garrett, with his protective personality and proper ways. He'd joined in on the toast, too, but now that it was over, he appeared to be analyzing Max. Was he questioning the validity of his story? Did he suspect the truth?

Max frowned. He didn't like being judged and especially not by a man who'd helped him fight his childhood battles. "Why are you looking at me like that?"

"Because I want you to say it one more time," Garrett replied.

"Say what?"

"That you're in love with Lizzie."

Shit, Max thought. *Shit.* He grabbed his champagne and took a swig, needing the buzz. "Why are you goading me to repeat myself?"

"I'm not goading you, little brother. I just want to hear you say it."

"I already did." And it had taken every ounce of strength inside him to rattle off those phony feelings. Topping it off, he was immersed in images of how Lizzie had looked when they talked about kissing at the wedding. Rubies and diamonds and dreamy musings. How was he supposed to deal with all that?

Jake put down his fork. He'd been enjoying his big old rib-eye steak, but now he watched Max and Garrett like a tennis match.

Garrett turned to Jake. "Does Max look like he's about ready to jump out that window to you?" He gestured to the view. The restaurant was on the tenth floor, overlooking the city.

"Actually, he does." A slow grin spread across Jake's face. "But I was like that, too, when I first realized how I felt about Carol."

"Ditto," Garrett said. "About Meagan."

Now Max wanted to wring both of their necks. Apparently, Garrett had only been kidding around, setting Max up and pulling Jake into it, too.

Max shook his head. Typically, Garrett wasn't a jokester. "When did you get to be such a wise guy?"

"Since you brought us here and told us you were getting married. But in all seriousness, I was surprised to hear it. I never thought you and Lizzie were anything more than friends." Garrett sat straight and tall in his chair, impeccable, as always. "But you already explained that the adoption brought you closer."

Just in case the lies weren't clear, Max reiterated, "We're not getting married because of the adoption. But it is part of the reason we scheduled the wedding so soon."

Jake interjected, "I had a short engagement, too. But that's what sometimes happens when children are involved."

Max managed a smile. "Oh, that's right. While I was on my sabbatical, searching for the meaning of life and volunteering at an orphanage, you were at a wild party in the Caribbean impregnating your assistant."

Jake chuckled. "It was just that one weekend. Speaking of which, are you and Lizzie planning a big family? Maybe more adoptions? Or a few seedlings of your own?"

Max all but blinked. They hadn't even gotten the first kid and already they were being prodded to have more? "We're just going to focus on Tokoni for now." It was as good an answer as any and certainly more diplomatic than admitting that they would be divorced long before the possibility of other children ever came up.

"I was panicked at first about becoming a dad." Jake returned to his steak, cutting into it again. "But not anymore. My wife and daughter are everything to me."

"I'm not scared of being a father." Max was thrilled about that. It was being Lizzie's husband that freaked him out. To combat those fears, he admitted, "I am a little anxious about the wedding." Before either of his brothers could question him, he chalked up his anxiety to being a rushed groom. "There's just so much to do in such a short amount of time. I'm glad you guys will be there, standing up for me." They'd already agreed to be his best men. He addressed Garrett. "Can you recommend a wedding planner? Maybe someone you use at the hotel or an associate of theirs?"

"Sure. I'll email you a list of names. And don't worry, it'll turn out great."

"It definitely will," Jake agreed. "But don't forget about the honeymoon, too."

Max quickly replied, "That's already been worked out. We'll be going back to Nulah to start the adoption proceedings. But we'll still get to hang out at the resort where we stayed before and enjoy the beach." Only on this trip, they would have to share a bungalow, like a husband and wife would be expected to do. And that was the part about being married that petrified him the most. Wanting Lizzie, he thought, more than he ever had before. But not being able to have her.

Within a week after getting engaged, Max and Lizzie hired a whirlwind of a planner who would be consulting with them at every turn. And if that wasn't enough to keep them busy, Max had decided to revamp his yard for the ceremony, with a custom gazebo surrounded by a garden. Lizzie already thought his yard made a stunning statement, with its parklike acreage, but now it was going to be even prettier. She walked beside him as he explained work that would soon be underway.

He said, "I told the landscaper I wanted something tropical. I showed him pictures of the private gardens at the resort in Nulah to give him a feel for what I'm after. I assumed that you would approve, since you incorporated that style onto your patio."

"I only dabbled with a few extra plants." Nonetheless, she was impressed that he'd noticed her effort.

He gestured in the distance. "They're going to build a stone walkway from the back of the house that curves around to the gazebo and serves as part of the wedding aisle. Then all the way around that will be the garden, with a waterfall fountain and some intricate little pathways."

"So essentially, we'll be getting married in the middle of the garden?" She gazed at the lawn, imagining the changes in her mind. Clearly, the landscaper and his crew would be working around the clock to complete the job. "It sounds spectacular."

"I figured if we're going to do it, we might as well do it right. I also thought it would make a nice spot for Tokoni later, for when he plays out here. It's too bad that coconut trees don't grow in this environment or I would add some of those, too."

"To give Tokoni a sense of home? We're going to have to take him back to Nulah for vacations so he doesn't lose his connection to it."

"We'll definitely do that, as often as we can." Max smiled. "I can't wait until he's our son."

"Me, too. It makes all this wedding stuff worthwhile." She breathed in the late-spring air. It would be summer by the time the ceremony took place. "I haven't talked to my dad yet. I haven't even told him that I'm getting married."

"You're going to have to do that soon, Lizzie."

"I know. But I haven't been completely remiss. I called my friends. Not everyone I associate with, but the ones I asked to be my bridesmaids. I spent an entire day on the phone, chatting with my gal pals and pretending to be in love." But she knew Max had done the same thing when he'd dined with his brothers. "It was interesting, how mixed the reactions were. Some of my friends were surprised, but others claimed that they knew all along that something was going on between us."

He checked her out, softly, slowly. "Funny, how people can't tell lust from love."

Her skin turned warm, her blood tingling in her body. "At least it's working in our favor."

He didn't respond. Instead, his stare got bolder, hungrier, as if he couldn't seem to help himself.

Lizzie's mouth went dry. If they were a real couple, heading into a genuine marriage, would they pull each other to the ground right here and now, desperate to make love on their future wedding site?

Pushing those dangerous thoughts out of her mind, she glanced away from him, breaking his stare.

He walked closer to where the gazebo was going to be, and she fell into step with him, eager to get past the heat that warmed her blood. But nonetheless, an inferno ensued. Clearly, he was still feeling it, too.

Finally, she started a new conversation by saying, "I chose blue, green and purple for the colors, with shades ranging from turquoise to magenta."

He squinted. "Colors?"

"For the wedding. It's called a peacock palette." She envisioned it being deep and rich and vibrant. "I spent hours on the net, looking at color combinations and kept coming back to that one. I hope that's all right with you."

"Sure." He stopped walking. "It sounds beautiful. I wonder what peacock symbolism is. I'm always interested in the spiritual meaning connected to animals."

She noticed how the sun shone upon his hair, creating blue-black effects. "That's the Lakota in you."

"Yes, I suppose it is." He removed his phone from his pocket. "Why don't I look it up right now?"

Still studying him, she waited while he did an internet search.

He shared the results with her. "First off, they're birds in the pheasant family, and only the male is referred to as a peacock. The female is a peahen, and both are peafowl. In terms of spirituality, some of the peacock and peahen's gifts include beauty, integrity and the ability to see into the past, present and future."

Fascinated by it all, she said, "That's quite a résumé."

"It's the eye shape on the feathers that gives them the gift of sight." He kept reading, explaining the meanings. "In relation to human spirituality, beauty and integrity is achieved when someone shows his or her true colors, so that's where all those colors come into play."

Suddenly Lizzie took pause, concerned about what he was saying and how it related to them. "Maybe we shouldn't use the peacock palette."

He glanced up from his phone. "Why not?"

"Because we're not showing our true colors. This whole thing is a lie."

"No, it isn't. Not if you look at it on a deeper scale. What we feel for Tokoni is our truth, our true colors, and adopting him is what our wedding is about to us." He glanced at his phone again. "It also says that peacocks have an association to resurrection, like the phoenix that rises out of the ashes. And isn't that what we're doing? Rising out of the ashes of our pasts and creating new lives for ourselves by becoming Tokoni's parents?"

When he lifted his gaze, she got caught up in the feeling, looking deeply into his eyes. "I'm so glad I'm going to share a child with you."

"Me, too, with you." He fell silent for a moment, looking as intently at her as she was at him. Then he asked, "So you're keeping the peacock palette, right?"

"Yes." She broke eye contact, needing to free herself from his spell. "I'm going to keep it."

"Do you think you could add a bit of gold?"

"Gold?" she parroted.

"To the color scheme. It would be cool if your dress had some gold on it."

He was putting in a special wardrobe request? Then it hit her. Lady Ari was wearing a gold dress in the painting he'd bought. "Do you want me to wear my hair loose, too?" Long and free and wild, like the goddess's?

"It would certainly look pretty that way." He reached out as if he meant to run his fingers through her hair, but he lowered his hand without doing it. "But that's up to you."

"I'll talk to my stylist about it and decide when the time comes." She didn't want to sound too eager to please him, not with how romantic he was making her feel. "What do you think of Ivy and Nita as the flower girls?" she asked, moving the discussion away from her and onto the people who would be part of procession. "Meagan and Carol could walk down the aisle with them. Meagan could hold Ivy's hand, and Carol could carry Nita."

"That's a great idea, having them participate in the ceremony, especially since my brothers are going to be in it, too."

"I'm having lunch with Meagan and Carol tomorrow, so I'll talk to them about it then. Meagan invited us to her house." No men, she thought, only women and children. But Max and his brothers had already had their meeting.

"So, what should we do about a ring bearer?" he asked. "Who should we get to do that?"

"I wish it could be Tokoni." Her heart swelled just thinking about him. "But Losa would never let us bring him to the States to be in our wedding." Tokoni didn't even know that she and Max planned to adopt him. He wouldn't be informed about his prospective parents until everything was approved.

"I wish it could be him, too," Max said.

"So maybe we'll just skip having a ring bearer?" She couldn't fathom having another boy in place of him.

Max agreed, then said, "We can have an adoption party for Tokoni later, like Garrett and Meagan did for Ivy. Also, I think in lieu of wedding gifts, we should ask our guests to donate to the orphanage."

"That's perfect." Exactly as it should be. Not only would their marriage serve as the catalyst for adopting Tokoni, it would benefit all the other children there, too.

Meagan, Carol and Lizzie gathered around a coffee table in the living room of the residence where Meagan lived with Garrett. The elegant beachfront home was located on a cliff that overlooked the hotel and resort he owned.

They'd already had lunch, a taco feast Meagan had cooked, and now Lizzie was analyzing her companions and thinking about what she'd learned about them so far.

Meagan looked soft and natural in a chambray shirt, faded jeans and pale beige cowboy boots. Her long silky hair was plaited into a single braid, hanging down the center of her back. Little Ivy was dressed in western wear, too, but her outfit was much fancier and in shades of pink.

Both mother and daughter loved horses. Garrett's resort offered horseback riding along the beach, making the activity easily accessible to them. In fact, Meagan still worked as a stable hand in the original job Garrett had given her when she was first released from prison, even though she was engaged to him now. She'd kept the job to pay back the restitution she owed and meet the requirements of her parole.

Lizzie glanced over at Carol, who was a lovely strawberry blonde with a curvy figure and sparkling green eyes. She still worked in her original job, too, as Jake's personal assistant. But nowadays, she and Jake had baby Nita to consider, so they took the infant with them to the office, where Jake had built an on-site nursery especially for their daughter. A nanny was also on hand to help. Lizzie thought it sounded like a wonderful setup.

Carol was a former foster kid who'd lost her family. In that sense, she and her husband shared tragic histories. But as youths, they'd handled their grief in opposing ways. While Jake was running wild, Carol compensated by being a bit too well behaved. Lizzie understood. She'd become an overly proper person herself.

She turned her attention to Carol's daughter. The baby was asleep in a carrier, with two-and-a-half-year-old Ivy sitting on the floor, watching her like a mother hen. Even if they weren't blood related, the children looked like cousins, with their dark hair, chubby cheeks and golden-brown skin.

Tokoni would fit right in, Lizzie thought. He was tailor-made for this group. She was certain that he was going to love being part of Max's foster family.

Even Lizzie was beginning to love it, with how warm and welcoming Meagan and Carol were being to her.

Would that change after the divorce, creating a divide between Lizzie and the other women, or wouldn't it matter, since she and Max intended to remain close once the marriage was over?

"Did Max take you shopping for your ring?" Carol

asked, drawing her into conversation. "Or did he choose it by himself?"

"We were together when he bought it," she replied. "But he picked it out."

"It's absolutely gorgeous." Carol leaned over to get a closer look. They were seated side by side on a comfy sofa, with a sweeping view of the ocean. "It's sexy for an engagement ring."

Fire and passion, Lizzie thought, burning deep within. "Max said it reminded him of my hair."

"I can see why." Carol smiled. "That ruby is perfect for you. I think all of our men did a great job of picking out our rings." She held out her hand. "Jake had mine made in the style of a Claddagh ring because my great-grandparents were from Ireland, and he wanted to honor my heritage. He gave it to me before I'd agreed to marry him because Claddagh rings can be worn if you're single, in a relationship, engaged or married. It depends which hand you wear it on and which way the crown at the top is facing. Mine is obviously in the married position now."

"What an interesting concept." Lizzie gazed at the ring. Along with the gold crown, it boasted a dazzling pink diamond in the shape of a heart being held by two engraved hands. The band itself was etched like a feather, a Native American detail that appeared to be woven into the Irish design. "It's very romantic."

Carol replied, "I didn't want to marry Jake at first because he was so opposed to falling in love. I loved him before he realized that he loved me."

"That happened to me, too," Meagan said. "I became aware of my feelings for Garrett before he recognized his for me. But with how complex our relationship was, we were both struggling with it."

Lizzie shifted on the sofa. According to the lie she and Max had concocted, they'd embraced their feelings at the same time.

Meagan continued by saying, "Garrett gave me a blue diamond in my engagement ring because I'm fascinated with blue roses. I learned about them through my sister-in-law. She studied a Victorian practice called the language of flowers, where couples used to send each other messages by using plants and flowers. Blue roses aren't found in nature, so they aren't part of the Victorian practice, but they've been introduced into the modern language of flowers."

Lizzie asked, "How did the people in the Victorian era know what the plants and flowers meant?"

"There were dictionaries on the subject. But there were different versions, so it could get confusing if they weren't using the same one."

Lizzie remarked, "Max hired a landscaper to plant a big beautiful garden for the wedding. We're having the ceremony in his backyard and the reception in his ballroom."

Meagan said, "You should research the language of flowers and have the landscaper plant some flowers that have meanings that would be special to you and Max."

Lizzie thought about Tokoni. He was the most special thing between her and Max. "Do you think there are flowers or plants that represent parenthood?"

"Oh, I'm sure there are. I'll bet you can find the information online. It's so exciting that you'll be adopting that little boy." Meagan grinned. "And I was right about you and Max becoming more than just friends."

Lizzie, of course, nodded in agreement, protecting the lie. But even so, the lie was starting to seem real, with how badly she wanted to kiss him. And hold him. And feel his body pressed tightly to hers.

Before she delved too deeply into that, she said to Carol and Meagan, "I would love to have your children in my wedding." She explained her idea about having Ivy and Nita as flowers girls, with their mothers accompanying them.

Both women accepted with joyful reactions, excited about the upcoming nuptials.

Afterward, Meagan said, "This will be the second time Ivy will be a flower girl. She was in my brother Tanner's wedding. But she's going to love sharing this one with Nita."

Ivy didn't bat an eye. She continued watching the baby sleep, even tucking a fluffy yellow teddy bear close to the infant.

"Nita means bear in Jake's ancestral tongue," Carol interjected. "We picked it because of all the teddy bears we've been given as gifts for her."

"She's a beautiful baby," Lizzie said, turning to study the kids again. "And so is Ivy's connection to her." It was such a tender scene, so sweet and loving that she knew she'd made the right choice by including the children and their mothers in the ceremony.

But Lizzie wasn't out of the woods yet. She still had to marry Max and fight her touchy-feely urges for him.

Eight

Lizzie glanced around her condo. Everything was in order, neat as a pin. The decorative pillows on her sofa were plumped. The magazines on the end tables were angled just so. She had a platter of fresh-cut fruit and gourmet cheeses in the fridge, along with a liter bottle of her dad's favorite soda. She'd invited him over today.

"I hate seeing you like this," Max said.

She turned to look at him. He'd come by for moral support, but he wasn't staying. He would be leaving before her dad arrived. "I'll be all right."

"Are you sure you don't want me to hang around?" He stood in the middle of her living room, his thumbs hooked in his jeans pockets. "We can both tell him about the wedding. After all, I am the guy you're going to marry."

"I think it's better for me to do this alone." She couldn't handle sitting there, pretending to be Max's fiancée in front of her father, not with how uncomfortably romantic this wedding was beginning to make her feel. "Besides, what's the point of you expending the energy to try to become his son-in-law when we'll just be getting divorced later?"

"We've been expending that type of energy for everyone else. And at least he already knows me." He crinkled his forehead. "I'll never forget the first time I met him."

"And how awkward it was?" When they were teenagers, she'd invited Max to the house for Christmas dinner, and the three of them had stumbled through a stilted conversation, with a big professionally decorated tree in the background. After Mama died, Dad always hired someone to dress the tree. But for Lizzie that just made the glittery ornaments and twinkling lights seem fake and lonely.

Sometimes, even now, she brought Max with her on that dreaded holiday, just so she didn't have to suffer through it by herself. Last Christmas was particularly odd. Rather than going to the house, they'd dined on a catered meal at Dad's high-rise office, before he'd jetted off for an overseas business trip, leaving her and Max alone for the rest of the day.

"Yeah, it's always awkward with your dad," he said. "But how often do you see him? Once, maybe twice a year?"

"I wish I didn't feel obligated to spend every dang Christmas with him." But it had become a painful ritual neither of them had broken.

Max sent her a concerned look. "Have you decided what you're going to do?"

"If I'm going to ask him to give me away?" She released an audible breath. It was a loaded question, filled with jittery bullets. "I have mixed feelings about it." Mixed and shaken. "I'm nervous about walking down the aisle by myself, so in that respect, it will be nice to have someone by my side. But with how distant my relationship is with him, will it even make a difference?"

"Whatever you choose to do, just remember that I'll be waiting for you at the altar."

Her temporary groom? Just thinking about kissing him at the wedding was already filling her with a flood of unwelcome warmth. She bit down on her bottom lip. This biting thing was becoming a habit.

Silent, he watched her.

She quickly said, "You'd better go. My dad will be here at two." And it was already one thirty. If anything, her father was highly punctual.

She walked Max outside, and when he leaned toward her, she panicked, her pulse pounding in her ears. He wasn't going to jump the gun and kiss her, was he? Now, like this?

She hurriedly asked, "What are you doing?"

"There's a ladybug behind you, and I want to see if it'll climb onto my finger. They're supposed to bring luck."

Good God. She glanced over her shoulder and saw the spotted beetle in question, perched on a shrub beside her door. "Sorry. I thought you were…"

"I was what?"

She turned back to face him, admitting the truth. "Going to kiss me."

"Today? While your dad is on his way over?" He glanced at her mouth, looking hot and restless and hungry. "Is that what you want me to do? Will that make it easier for you?"

She bit her lip again, chewing on her lipstick, struggling to contain her desire for him. "I think we should wait until the ceremony like we're supposed to."

He stepped back, away from the ladybug, away from her. "The gazebo. The garden. You in a long white gown."

The wedding that was messing with their heads, she thought. "I have an appointment later this week to try on dresses. It's at an exclusive bridal salon some of my friends have used. I told the owner that you want me to wear a dress with gold embellishments, so they've been gathering gowns from designers all over the world to fulfill your request."

"Really? That's awesome, Lizzie. But remember that I'm paying for everything, okay? So don't spare any expense."

And buy the best gown she could find? "I'm going to try to look the way you want me to look."

"You're always beautiful to me. I think about you all the time. In the morning when I wake up. When

I'm in the shower. When I'm working. When I go to bed at night. It's frustrating, knowing you're going to be my bride."

He meant sexually frustrating, she thought. And she understood exactly how he felt. "I think about you all the time, too."

"The way I've been thinking about you?"

"Yes." She crossed her arms over her chest, trying to stop her heart from leaping into her throat.

He shifted his stance, the air between them getting thicker. "This is wrong, isn't it?"

To be torturing themselves this way? To be pushing the boundaries of their friendship? "We're supposed to know better."

He glanced toward his car, a luxury hybrid parked on the street. "I should leave now and let you get on with your day."

She nodded. They certainly couldn't remain where they were, saying intimate things to each other.

But instead of shutting him out of her thoughts, she watched him walk away, dazed by her appetite for him.

Forcing air into her lungs, Lizzie returned to the house to wait for her dad.

He arrived sharply at two. Stiff and formal, David McQueen was a tall, trim man with an impeccable posture. As always, his short graying red hair was neatly trimmed. He wore a conservative blue suit and pin-striped tie. She assumed that he'd just come from a business meeting. Even before Lizzie's mom died, he was a workaholic. But at least they'd been a family then. Sometimes he even waltzed around the parlor with Mama, bowing to her after each dance. Lizzie used to sneak down the stairs and watch her parents, fascinated by how good they looked together.

Clearing her mind, she placed the snack tray on the coffee table, with small serving plates and paper napkins. She offered him a glass of soda, over ice. He used a coaster for his drink. He always did. Dad wouldn't think of leaving damp marks on a table.

He thanked her and said, "You didn't have to go to all this trouble for me."

He put a few bite-size pieces of cheese on a plate. He took a handful of grapes, too, and some watermelon balls. A polite amount of food, she thought.

She sat across from him. Since he'd claimed the sofa, she went for a leather recliner. When she'd invited him to come over, she told him that she had something important to discuss with him. Most likely, he was waiting for her to get started. Dad wasn't one for small talk. Mama had been. She could chat about insignificant things for hours.

But at the very end, Mama's words were few. The only thing she'd written on the notepad beside her bed on that fateful day was *I'm sorry. Please be happy without me.*

Lizzie gazed across the coffee table at her dad. *Happy* wasn't part of his vocabulary. It hadn't been part of hers, either, not after she'd become a motherless child.

Their housekeeper had found the body and the

note. Mama had done the deed while Dad was at work and Lizzie was at school.

"I'm getting married," she said, going right for her news.

Dad calmly replied, "I noticed the ruby on your finger when I first got here, but I didn't want to say anything in case it wasn't an engagement ring. But apparently it is." He paused. "Who's the lucky man?"

"It's Max."

"I'm glad to hear it."

"You are?" She hadn't expected him to express his opinion, least of all his approval. Normally, Dad remained neutral when it came to Lizzie's life. Then again, he'd said it in his usual cut-and-dried way.

"It never made sense to me that you weren't dating him. You two seem so suited. But it appears you both figured that out."

Lizzie nodded, playing her part as Max's fiancée. But still, she'd never suspected that her father had been analyzing her friendship with Max all this time. "It's going to be at his house, on the second Saturday in June. I'm sorry for the short notice, but we're anxious to make it happen. I hope the date isn't a problem for you, with your work schedule," she clarified.

He sat back in his seat. "Of course not. I wouldn't miss my daughter's wedding."

Well, okay, then. At least he'd confirmed that he would be there. Now on to the next phase, she thought, the next question. "Do you want to walk me down the aisle?"

"Certainly." He sipped his soda. "I'd be honored."

Did he mean that? Or was it merely the proper thing to say? With him, it was hard to tell. "Just so you know, Dad, there's a child who's part of this."

His eyes went wide. The most emotion he'd showed yet. "You're pregnant?"

"Oh, my goodness. No. I didn't mean..." Based on the fact that she'd never even slept with Max, she thought about how impossible that would have been. "We're adopting a child. A five-year-old boy from Nulah."

"The one you wrote about on your blog?"

She angled her head. "You read my blog?"

"Sometimes."

They barely communicated, but he took the time to read her work? Her father was full of surprises.

"So is he the one?" he asked again.

"Yes. It's the same child who was featured on my blog." She explained how Max had gotten close to Tokoni when he volunteered at the orphanage last year. "Then he brought me to meet Tokoni and I bonded with him, too. We're excited about making him our son." She backtracked a little. "We haven't started the adoption proceedings, but we're going to do that after the wedding."

He studied her, with eyes the same shade of blue as hers. "You'll be a good mother, Elizabeth." He quietly added, "A good wife to Max, too."

Her father was buying into her marriage, just as everyone else had done. But lying to him seemed worse. Was it because he was the only human connection she had to her mom?

I'm so sorry. Be happy without me.

Now wasn't the time to think about Mama's final farewell. But she couldn't seem to stop herself from feeling the brunt of it. "Max has always been there when I need him," she heard herself say.

Dad reached for a piece of fruit off his plate, lifting it slowly, methodically, before he ate it. "The man you marry should be there for you."

His words struck a chord. Was he blaming himself for not being there for Mama? She wanted to know what he was thinking and feeling, but she didn't have the strength to ask him. And especially not while she was sitting there, pretending that her marriage was going to be real.

Dad didn't stay long. Within no time, they wrapped things up and she walked him outside, just as she'd done with Max earlier.

"I'll keep in touch about the wedding," she said as they stood in her courtyard. "Your tuxedo, the rehearsal dinner, all that stuff."

"Tell Max how pleased I am that you two got together."

"I will." She forced a smile. "Take care."

"You, too." He gave her a pat-on-the-back hug, which was about as affectionate as he got.

After they parted ways, she returned to the house, steeped in the complications of becoming Max's wife.

Lizzie's appointment at the bridal salon was private. Being as upscale as it was, it catered to a high-end clientele and offered preferential treatment.

She'd asked Meagan and Carol to join her, and now the three of them gathered in the lavishly decorated salon, sipping Dom Pérignon from crystal flutes. They'd been offered caviar and crackers, too, but they'd declined the salty appetizer. Personally, Lizzie had never acquired a taste for it.

She glanced at her companions, glad they were here. She couldn't do this alone, not with how overwhelmed she was. She wanted them to accompany her because they were part of Max's family, and, today of all days, she needed a family connection, with as often as she'd been thinking about her mom. Her father saying that she would make a good wife triggered her emotions, too, making everything seem far too real.

The salon had arranged for a showing, with models wearing the gowns that had been selected for her. She'd already been given a keepsake pen and a printed program, so she could checkmark the styles that appealed to her.

She sat in a wingback chair, with Meagan and Carol by her side, and watched the models emerge.

Every dress was exquisite in its own way, but there was one that drew Lizzie into its long, flowing silk-and-lace allure. The creation offered a magical silhouette, embellished with crystal jewels and iridescent gold beads. A richly appliquéd bodice and chapel train with a French bustle lent the gown a sensual appeal.

Even Meagan and Carol gasped when they saw it.

Lizzie imagined it with a peacock-palette bouquet and her hair tumbling in thick red waves.

"Look how romantic that is," Carol said.

Yes, Lizzie thought. It was like something out of a wedding night fantasy. She even envisioned Max sweeping her into his arms and carrying her straight to his bed.

His bed?

She shivered from the forbidden thought. She wasn't supposed to be dwelling on her desire for Max. But she couldn't seem to control the ache it caused.

She drank more champagne, trying to cool off. But it didn't do any good. Daydreaming about the man she was going to marry swirled through her blood, heating her from the inside out.

"Are you going to mark that dress?" Meagan asked her.

Lizzie snapped to attention. "Yes." She was eager to try it on, hoping it looked as enchanting on her as it did on the model.

She marked other gowns, as well. But her mind kept drifting back to the fantasy one.

Finally, after the show ended, she was escorted to a luxurious fitting room. Meagan and Carol came with her.

The fantasy gown was incredible. With the beautiful way the gold beads reflected the light, she looked like a princess.

Or a fire-tinged goddess, she surmised, like the

painting of Lady Ari. But that was the point. The reason Max wanted her gown to be marked with gold.

"You look absolutely radiant," Meagan said. "Like a bride should."

A bride who was desperate for her groom. Lizzie squeezed her eyes shut, making her reflection disappear. But when she opened her eyes, the hungry woman in the glittering gown was still there.

Suddenly, she was afraid of how easily she'd found a dress, of how it seemed to be made just for her. "This is how it was when Max chose my ring for me."

Too right, she thought. Too perfect.

Meagan and Carol smiled, assuming she meant it in a good way. But there was nothing good about how badly she wanted to be with Max.

Two weeks before the wedding, Max awakened in a cold sweat. He sat up in bed and dragged a hand through his hair.

The closer he got to saying, "I do," the more restless he became. Hunger. Desire. Lust. He had it bad, so damned bad. Getting naked with Lizzie was all he thought about, dreamed about, fantasized about.

He blew out the breath in his lungs. He knew what she looked like in a bikini, with her tantalizing cleavage and pierced navel. But he'd never seen her completely bare.

Were her nipples a soft shade of pink? Did they arouse easily? Would she sigh and moan if he rolled his tongue across them? He wondered all sorts of erotic things about her. Was she smooth between her legs or did she have a strip of fiery red hair? And what would she do if he kissed her there?

Right *there*, all warm and soft and wet.

He longed to kiss her everywhere, to hold her unbearably close, to feel the silkiness of her skin next to his.

He'd wanted her for years, and now that they were getting married, the wanting had taken on a new meaning.

The romance of making love with his wife.

Cripes, he thought. Since when did he care about romance? Max was out of his element, with the effect the impending marriage was having on him. But it would be over soon enough. After they adopted Tokoni, they would get happily divorced and everything would go back to normal.

But in the meantime...

He squinted at the light peeking through the blinds. It was the crack of dawn and he needed to get up and get moving. Lizzie was coming by later this morning to see the garden. The work was finished, the gazebo built and ready.

Was it any wonder he was stressed? A day hadn't passed where there wasn't something related to the wedding. Sure, the planner was doing a bang-up job of getting everything done. But it was still consuming Max's life.

And so was his yearning for Lizzie.

He climbed out of bed and put his running clothes on, anxious to hightail it out of his house.

And that was exactly what he did. He ran through the canyons, taking in the crisp morning air. He worked up an even bigger sweat than the one that had drenched him during the night.

By the time he was done, he was ready for a long, water-pummeling, soap-sudsy shower. Of course, once he was naked, he thought about Lizzie again. But at least he didn't touch himself. That would have made the wanting so much worse.

After he got dressed and ate breakfast, he went out to the garden to wait for Lizzie. He'd already opened the security gate so she could let herself onto the property.

She arrived with her hair falling over her shoulders and a breezy blouse flowing over a pair of slim-fitting jeans. He wanted to ravish her right then and there.

"Look at this place," she said as she approached him. "It's absolutely gorgeous."

"Glad you like it."

"Like it? I love it. It's like the Garden of Eden."

The last thing he wanted to think about was a biblical paradise, where temptation ran amok. If Lizzie presented him with an apple, he would devour every luscious bite.

"Max?"

He blinked at her. "What?"

"Are we going to walk through it so I can see everything up close?"

"Yes, of course." The design was lush and dense, surrounded by stately palms and giant birds of paradise. Vertical layers of plants and flowers created a junglelike appearance within a bold, brightly colored interior.

They wandered the variegated pathways, then stopped to admire the fountain, listening to the rainlike sound it made.

Next, they headed for the gazebo and stood inside the custom-built structure. It wasn't decorated for the wedding yet, but when the time came, it would be adorned with flowers and sheer linen drapes.

"This is where it's going to happen," she said.

Yeah, he thought. Where he would marry the woman he longed to bed. But at least he would get to kiss her.

"So, how are things going on your end?" he asked, trying to shake the anticipated kiss from his mind. "Do all the women in the bridal party have their dresses and whatnot?"

"Yes, they do. I decided on mismatched dresses, with each of them choosing what looked best on them. I wanted them to express their individuality instead of putting everyone in the same style. My only stipulation was that they remained within the color theme."

"Are you pleased with the dress you got for yourself?" With as much time as they'd spent talking about it, he was eager to see her in it.

"Truthfully, it makes me feel a little strange."

He angled his head. "Strange?"

She winced. "Just sort of wedding nightish, with how soft and pretty it is."

Damn, he thought. *Damn.* "I guess it's too late to trade it in for an ugly one, huh?"

She smiled, laughed a little. "Now, why didn't I think of that?"

He doubted that it would make a difference. He slid his gaze over her and asked, "Did you have to get special lingerie to go with it?" He didn't have a clue what brides wore under their gowns.

She flushed in the sunlight, her fair skin going far too pink. "We're doing it again, Max."

He frowned. "Doing what?"

"Saying things to each other we shouldn't say." She fussed with the buttons on her blouse, as if they might accidentally come undone. "We need to change the subject."

His brain went blank. "To what?"

"I don't know."

He hurriedly thought of something. He gestured to a small section of the garden. "See that area over there?"

She glanced in the direction of where he pointed. "Yes."

"Those are the plants that were added for the language of flowers you told me about. I asked the landscaper to research it and he worked up a collection of flowers that pertain to joy and parenthood and welcoming a new son."

"Oh." She made a soft sound. "That's wonderful. Thank you."

"You're welcome. We'll have to tell Tokoni about it when he comes here."

"He's going to love this garden." She gasped. "Oh, my goodness, look. It's a ladybug." She showed him where the little creature was crawling on a railing of the gazebo. "Do you want to see if it'll come to you?"

"Sure." He went over to the ladybug and held his hand close to it. Sure enough, it crawled onto his finger.

She watched the exchange. "I wondered if they bring a specific type of luck or if it's general goodwill."

"I don't know. I'll look it up after it flies away."

Just then the ladybug winged its way toward Lizzie and landed on the back of her hand.

She smiled and glanced down at it. "This has to be a good omen, right?"

Finally the beetle took off, disappearing into the garden. Curious, Max got on his phone to research the luck they'd just been given.

"What does it say?" she asked.

"There's lots of information. They mean different things in different cultures. But get this—in one of the old myths, if a ladybug lands on a woman's hand, it means she is going to be married soon."

"Oh, wow. Imagine that? Does it say anything about a ladybug landing on a man's hand?"

He scanned the material. "There is something here about…" Oh, shit, he thought, as he read the contents. "Never mind. It doesn't matter."

She scrunched up her face. "It's not something about the wedding night, is it?"

"No." He frowned at his phone. "It's about love.

It says, 'The direction in which a ladybug flies away from a man's hand is where his true love will be.'"

He glanced up, and they gazed at each other with disturbed expressions. The ladybug hadn't just flown in Lizzie's direction. It had gone right to her, making her his supposed true love.

But Max refused to believe a message like that, especially when there were other ways to analyze it.

"I'll bet the ladybug is part of our lie," he said. "That it's aware of the reason we've been pretending to be in love and is playing along with us."

A strand of hair blew across her cheek. She batted it away without saying anything. She still seemed a little dazed.

He prodded her for a response. "Don't you think my theory sounds logical, Lizzie?"

"Yes." She walked out of the gazebo, her hair still blowing. "That has to be it. It's the only thing that makes sense."

"Definitely," he said as they left the garden. They both knew that neither of them had the capacity to fall in love for real.

Nine

On the day of the wedding, Lizzie clutched her father's arm. Within a matter of minutes, she would be walking down the garden-path aisle, heading toward her groom.

Max Marquez. Her best friend. The man with whom she would be adopting a child.

She glanced over at her dad. Surprisingly, his strong and silent presence helped keep her limbs from shaking. But the storm that raged through her mind was a whole other matter.

Ever since the ladybug incident, she'd been struggling with the dangling, tangling heartstrings of love. Max's explanation that the ladybug's message was part of their lie should have satisfied her. But instead she'd begun worrying about love, fearful that it could happen to her.

Anxious, Lizzie looked down at her bouquet. At the moment, she was wearing blue, green and purple diamond earrings that complemented the colors of the flowers. Max had given the earrings to her as a wedding gift. They'd been specially made for this occasion.

She'd given him a jewelry gift, too: antique gold cuff links to wear with his tuxedo. Of course, once the ceremony was underway, she would be placing the band she'd chosen for him on his finger.

As for her rings, her engagement ruby and diamond pavé band had been soldered together to create one shimmering piece, and that was what Max would be marrying her with today.

She shifted her gaze to the elegantly decorated gazebo, where he waited for her. Soon, so very soon, she would be his legally wedded wife. She'd never believed herself capable of love, and now she was fretting over it. But given how long she'd known Max and as close as they'd always been, weren't those types of feelings possible?

As the opening notes of "Here Comes the Bride" began to play, signaling her entrance, she lifted her chin, determined to stay strong.

Her father glanced over and said, "It's time."

She nodded. Everyone, including Max, turned to watch her come down the aisle. But she doubted that he was worried about love. He seemed fixated on how she looked, his appreciative gaze sweeping the long, silky, white-and-gold length of her.

She shouldn't have told him that her dress made her feel "wedding nightish." But she couldn't take those words back. She couldn't take any of this back. She was marrying Max and afraid that she might fall hopelessly in love with him.

Would she know the moment it occurred? Would it pierce her like a warrior's arrow? Or would it be a gradual wound, a slow bleeding with an eventual loss of consciousness?

Lizzie held her breath, praying that her heart remained intact. Because nothing would tear her apart more than loving a man she was destined to divorce.

As her dad turned her over to Max, she wished that she'd worn a veil to cover her face. She felt terribly exposed, with the passion-steeped way Max was looking at her.

She gazed longingly at him, too, mesmerized by his tall, dark beauty. He wore his hair in its usual style, as thick and shiny and straight as it naturally was. His designer tuxedo featured satin details and notched lapels, and his boutonniere was attached on the left side, above his heart, where it was supposed to be.

He recited his vows first, as instructed to do. As he promised to love and honor her for all eternity, a soft rattle sounded in his voice. She recited hers just as quietly, just as shakily. Only her vows were rife with fear.

They exchanged rings, and when the time came

for him to kiss her, Lizzie refrained from running her tongue across her lips. But that didn't ease the romantic restlessness that baited her soul. She was wearing red lipstick, as hot and fiery as the rubies in their rings.

"Are you ready?" he whispered.

"Yes," she said. She was more than ready.

He leaned forward and put his hands in her hair. His lips touched hers, and her eyes fluttered closed. This was the kiss she'd been thinking about, fantasizing about, waiting for. He pulled her closer, and the elements flowed through her.

The sun. The wind. The bloom of flowers.

Was she becoming part of her surroundings? Or did she feel this way because she was becoming part of him?

Lizzie couldn't think clearly, not while she was in the dreamy midst of wanting him. He didn't use his tongue and neither did she, but it still felt beautifully forbidden.

It ended far too soon, with him separating himself from her. She opened her eyes. His were open now, too.

Her mind went hazy. Was her lipstick smeared? Max didn't have any on him, so it must be okay. It was supposed to be the long-lasting, non-smudge kind. For infinite kisses, she thought.

The ceremony came to a close, with the man officiating it introducing them as husband and wife.

"We did it," Max said to her, his voice seductively quiet.

"Yes, we did," she murmured back. They were married now, first kiss and all.

As they descended the aisle, they were celebrated with cheers and the fragrant tossing of dried lavender. It dusted them like confetti, purple buds sprinkling the air. The wedding planner had recommended it, providing little mesh bags to their guests. Lizzie hadn't thought to check on what lavender meant in the language of flowers until last night, discovering that, among other things, it was said to soothe passions of the heart.

But as Max held her hand, his fingers threaded through hers, she wasn't the least bit soothed.

His touch only heightened her fears about falling in love.

The chandeliers in the ballroom had been altered, the original crystals replaced to reflect the colors of the wedding. Also enriching the décor were fancy linens, glittering candles and big, bold flower arrangements trimmed in peacock feathers.

The cake was outstanding, too. Max could see it from where he sat, displayed on a dessert cart, the four-tiered creation a frothily iced masterpiece. But for now he and Lizzie and their guests dined on their meals, prepared by a renowned chef and served on shiny gold plates.

Their table consisted of the wedding party. The best men and maid of honor had already made their toasts, and the flower girls and their mothers looked exceptional in their feminine finery. Baby Nita's nanny was part of the group, ready to whisk her off to a makeshift nursery that had been provided, in case the wee one needed a nap. A playroom for the older kids was also available, with child-care attendants standing by.

Lizzie's father fit naturally into the high-society gathering. He didn't seem as detached as he normally was, and for that Max was grateful. He wanted Lizzie to feel protected by her one and only parent, especially today. Watching her come down the aisle with her dad had left Max with a lump in his throat.

Becoming Lizzie's husband was confusing. The weight of the ring on his finger. The fake vows. The bachelorhood he'd lost. The make-believe wife he'd gained.

Earlier someone had imposed a "kiss and clink" ritual, where the bride and groom had to kiss whenever glasses were clinked together. So far, at the reception, Max and Lizzie had locked lips at least ten times. But he could have kissed her a thousand times and not gotten enough.

He leaned over and said to her, "Is it okay if I tell you again how beautiful you look?" He'd already told her how breathtaking she was, but he thought it bore repeating.

She softly replied, "You can say whatever you want, as often as you want."

"Then I'm going to say it every chance I get." With her sparkling gown and wild red hair, she was a seductive sight to behold. He wanted to haul her off to bed tonight, to strip her bare and relish every part of her. But that wasn't part of the arrangement.

In the next alluring moment, a whole bunch of glasses clinked in the background. Max hastily obliged. He cupped Lizzie's face and slanted his mouth over hers.

He'd yet to use his tongue. He wanted to, but it didn't seem appropriate with everyone watching. Still, he made sure that his lips were parted, just enough to entice a sigh from Lizzie.

No one would ever suspect that they weren't lovers. But Max knew. He craved her with every breath in his body.

Later, they engaged in their first husband-and-wife dance, with a well-known DJ spinning records. They'd chosen Queen's "You're my Best Friend," a classic soft rock ballad, for the opening song. Some of the lyrics included professions of love. But this was a wedding, and they were supposed to be projecting that type of sentiment, even if it wasn't true. Mostly, though, the song made sense, with how deep their friendship was.

As they swayed to the beat, holding each other close, Max ran his hand along the back of her gown, where it laced like an old-fashioned corset.

"Was it hard getting into your dress?" he asked.

She shook her head. "Sheila helped me."

Of course, he thought, her maid of honor, who was one of her old sorority sisters, a high-society girl, much like Lizzie. "She's probably used to dealing with these types of events."

"Yes, she is. But I had a team of assistants, too, a hairdresser, a makeup artist, a manicurist."

Max had gotten ready by himself. He hadn't wanted anyone, not even his brothers, straightening his tie or pinning his boutonniere to his lapel. He'd needed to spend his last few hours of being single alone. "Who's going to help you get out of your dress?"

"I can do it myself." She spoke quietly, with the colors from the chandeliers raining down on her. "I just have to be careful not to damage it."

He looked into her eyes, curious about what she had on under it—the mysterious lingerie that kept invading his mind. "You can come to me if the laces give you any trouble."

She nearly stumbled against him. "Do you think that's a good idea?"

"I don't know." He steadied her in his arms, wondering what the hell he was doing. He'd just invited her to his room, crossing a line that wasn't meant to be crossed. "I honestly don't." He couldn't be sure what would happen if they gave in to the temptation of being together. Would they regret it afterward, would they survive the heat? They'd been so careful not to jeopardize their friendship, and now they were drowning in a sea of unholy matrimony. "Maybe we should both forget that I ever suggested it."

"Yes," she agreed. "We should block it out."

He was trying. But the back of her dress kept getting in the way. He couldn't seem to stop from touching it.

The reception continued, with dancing and drinking and party merriment. During the removal of the garter, Max knelt beside Lizzie's chair, asking the Creator to give him the strength to endure it.

He'd been obsessing about her lingerie, and now he was getting to cop a husbandly feel of her sheer white stockings. They were the kind that stayed up all by themselves.

No hooks, no fasteners.

While he was still on the floor, with his hand lingering on her thigh, Jake called out, "Hey, Max, did you know that in earlier, bawdier times, wedding guests used to follow the couple to their bedchamber and wait for them to undress so they could steal the bride's stockings and toss them at her and the groom until they hit one of them in the head?"

"That's not funny," Max called back, even if he and Lizzie laughed right along with everyone else.

"It was for luck," Jake assured him.

Yeah, Max thought, because at least the old-time groom had been lucky enough to bed his bride, even if one of them had gotten softly pelted in the head.

As he looked up to meet Lizzie's gaze, preparing to slide the garter down, a group of jovial guests clinked glasses, daring him to kiss the graceful sweep of her leg.

Accepting the challenge, he pressed his lips to her ankle, being as gentlemanly as the moment would allow. But damned if he still didn't want to peel off every jeweled-and-beaded stitch of fabric she wore.

By the time Max and Lizzie cut the cake, the sexy

tone had already been set. He fed her a piece of the frothy white dessert, and when some banana-cream filling stuck lusciously to her lips, he leaned forward and kissed it right off her mouth.

Holy. Mercy. Hell.

She returned his salacious kiss, with camera phones flashing and recording every detail. For better or worse, Max felt wildly, sinfully married, their tongues meeting and mating.

Logic flew straight out the door. Desperate to have her, he whispered hotly in her ear, "Come to my room later and let me undo your dress," repeating his earlier offer and meaning every word of it.

Although Lizzie went beautifully breathy, she didn't respond, leaving Max waiting and wondering if his wife would succumb to his request.

Or leave him hanging.

The mansion was empty, the guests and staff gone. There was no one left, except Max and Lizzie. They stood on the second-floor landing, silence between them. In one direction was the master suite and in the other were her accommodations. She stalled, not knowing which way to go.

He watched her through pitch-dark eyes. In the low-level light, they looked as black as his licorice-toned hair.

So deep. So intense.

She struggled to tame her desire. "Sleeping with you wasn't supposed to be an option."

His gaze didn't waver. "It doesn't have to affect our friendship, not if we don't let it."

"How?" she asked. "By only doing it this one time and never again?"

"That seems like the safest way to handle it." He moved a little closer. "But it's up to you, Lizzie."

There was nothing safe about how much she wanted him. Or about the fear of love that kept burrowing its way into her thoughts. If she told him what was going on in her mind, would he still be willing to go through with it?

"I can't," she said, fighting the feeling. "No matter how much I want to."

"Are you sure?" Roughness edged his voice: loss, disappointment.

She nodded, trying her darnedest to be certain.

He said, "Then sleep well and think of me, and I'll think of you, too."

She imagined him, alone in his bed, fantasizing about her. "I better go." Before she crawled all over him. She could still taste the cake they'd kissed from each other's lips.

The sweet creaminess.

Lizzie turned away, but he didn't. She sensed him, standing in the same spot, tall and sharp in his tuxedo.

She headed toward the guest wing. Again, there was no movement behind her, no masculine footsteps, echoing in her ears. He remained as motionless as a statue.

She stopped to breathe, and when she glanced over her shoulder, she lost her reason.

He was still there.

Lizzie ran to him, her dress swishing with every beat of her bride-in-jeopardy heart. He pulled her tight against him, lifted her up and carried her the rest of the way to his room.

She kept her arms looped around his neck, hoping she survived the night without falling in love with him.

He took her into his suite, past a royal blue sitting room and into the area where a big brass bed took precedence. This was the place where he slept each night, she thought, where he dreamed, where they would be together.

"Just this once," she said, stating the rules, making sure she repeated them. "Then never again."

"Yes," he replied, putting her on her feet. "This is the only time it's going to happen." He moved to stand behind her. "On our wedding night."

She felt his hands on the back of her dress, working the ties. Wonderfully dizzy, her vision nearly blurred.

He loosened more of the fabric. "It's so soft and pretty."

"The material between my skin and the dress is called a modesty panel." But she wasn't feeling very modest. Soon she would be half-naked. The only garments she had on underneath were lace panties and the thigh-high stockings he'd run his hands over earlier. Her gown had been structured so she didn't need a bra.

Still standing behind her, he helped her remove

the dress, allowing her to step out of it. She didn't turn around, and he didn't ask her to. But she heard his sharp intake of breath as he closed in on her. Lizzie shivered, immersed in his nearness, while he skimmed his fingers along her spine.

"Look how bare you are," he said, following the line of her tailbone.

Yes, she thought. With her upper half clothes-free and only a wisp of lower lingerie, she was mostly bare.

Remaining where he was, directly behind her, Max circled her waist and reach around to the front of her panties. When he slipped a hand inside to cup her mound, she gasped on contact.

"You're smooth," he said, his voice raspy against her ear. "I've thought a lot about…"

The style of bikini wax she favored? She leaned back against him, stunned by how detailed his curiosity was. "You wondered about that?"

"All the time." He kept touching her, moving farther down, until he spread her open with the tips of his fingers.

Lizzie nearly came on the spot.

He rubbed her, teasing her, making her warm and slick and wet. He used his other arm to hold her in place, pressing it firmly across her breasts. Her nipples went unbearably hard.

There was something dominantly provocative about what he was doing and how he was doing it. He had all the power.

Her groom. Her husband.

She couldn't see his expression or the flashes of

heat that she suspected were in his eyes. But she felt every insistent touch.

"Are you going to come for me, Lizzie?"

She gulped her next breath. "I almost did."

"Yes, but are you going to do it for real?"

She nodded, as he continued his intimate quest, using her as his bridal plaything.

"This is just the beginning," he said.

"Of what?" she asked, feeling deliciously dazed.

"Of how many times tonight I'm going to make you come."

Her heart raced, spinning through her body like a top. "When am I going to get to do things to you?"

"You already are." He bumped his fly against her rear, showing her how aroused he was. "But I'm not anywhere near being done with you, so that will have to wait."

She closed her eyes. Every second of his stimulation brought her closer to the countless times he promised to invoke pleasure.

Lizzie moaned. Was the arm around her breasts getting tighter? Were his fingers strumming harder and faster? He kept his hand inside her panties, creating massive amounts of friction.

Her dress was on the floor beside their feet, so close they could have stepped on it. But neither of them did, not even when she came.

She convulsed in a flood of carnal bliss, shimmering and shaking, the back of her body banded against the front of his.

He nuzzled her neck and said, "Let's take these off now, shall we?"

She wondered what he meant, until she realized that he was talking about her panties. Blinking through the haze, she did her shaky best to recover.

He divested her of what remained: the panties in question, her shoes, her stockings, even the colorful diamond earrings he'd given her. He did all that while he was still standing behind her.

After there was nothing left to remove, he turned her around so he could view her nakedness.

"Damn," he said. "You're even more gorgeous than I imagined."

She couldn't think of a response, at least not one that wouldn't leave her mewling like a kitten at his feet. He was still fully clothed. If this was strip poker, she would have lost the moment he'd unlaced her gown.

He spoke once again. "I want you to turn down the covers and get into bed."

So he could finish what he started? She was eager to do his bidding, but nervous about it, too. He was looking at her as if he meant to hold her captive for the rest of her life.

But she knew that wasn't the case. Tonight was their only night. The only time they'd agreed to be together.

Wondering what it would be like to stay with him, to be his forever wife, she fought her fears, reminding herself that this was just sex—hot, dreamy sex—where love had nothing to do with it.

Ten

Max gazed at Lizzie, gloriously naked in his bed, with her hair tumbling over her shoulders and the soldered ring set that sealed their union glinting on her finger. She looked as much like a bride now as when she'd walked down the aisle. Wilder, he thought, more sensual, but a bride just the same.

He picked up her dress and placed it on a nearby chair, along with her panties and stockings and earrings. The only item left on the floor was her shoes. They weren't glass slippers, but they had a fairy-tale quality nonetheless. The entire wedding had seemed that way. Which was part of its allure, part of how it had been designed, he thought, fooling their guests into believing it was going to last forever.

And now he and Lizzie were alone, immersed in

one married night of romance. The anticipation in her eyes excited him. And so did her ladylike moments of shyness.

"Don't cover up," he told her, when she began to pull the sheet over her body.

She released it, giving him an unobstructed view once again. Mesmerized, he stood where he was, drinking in every beautifully bare part of her. Her nipples were as pink and pretty as he'd imagined, and his fingers were still warm from where he'd touched her.

Finally, Max removed his tux and draped it over the back of the same chair where he'd placed her dress.

"I never knew you were so meticulous," she said.

"Normally, I'm not." By tomorrow, the careful placement of their clothes wouldn't matter. But for now it did.

Once he was naked, he joined her in bed and took her in his arms. He kissed her with gentle passion, and she roamed her hands over him, her glitter-polished nails skimming the ridged planes and sinewy muscles that formed his body.

She paused when she came to a scar, a cigarette burn—a pale circular mark of childhood torture. Although the majority of them had disappeared, some of the deeper ones, mostly on his chest, remained visible.

"Max?" Still lingering over the scar, she lifted her gaze to his, her voice soft and compassionate. "Have other women asked you about these?"

"Yes." Other women, other lovers. "But I've never told them what they are. I just tell them what I tell everyone who is curious enough to question me about them. That I had a bad case of measles when I was a kid that left me scarred."

"Oh, yes, of course. Your measles tale. I always thought that seemed like a believable story, even if I knew the truth."

Max nodded. Lizzie was privy to the pain his mother had inflicted on him because he'd shared those gut-wrenching secrets with her.

"I'm so sorry for what she did to you," she said.

"I know you are." She'd told him that many times before. But hearing her say it now distressed him. He didn't want to be reminded of the abuse, not while they were being intimate. He moved her hand away from his scar, imploring her to stop touching it, letting her know it was off-limits.

A wounded look came into her eyes. Clearly, she wanted to comfort him, to do what she'd always done before. But Max couldn't bear to accept what she was offering.

When he turned down the bedside lamp, trying to shift gears and create a softer ambience, she asked, "Are you sure that being together like this isn't going to affect our friendship?"

"We can't let it," he said, even if a change was happening already. A discomfort he couldn't deny. But there was more at stake, he thought, than just the two of them. "We're going to co-parent a child. He's going to need us to stay close."

"But not this close," she said.

He climbed on top of her, preparing to kiss his way down her body, to turn their troubled closeness into mindless pleasure. "Everything will be okay, Lizzie."

"Promise?"

"Yes." Max licked her nipples, going back and forth, exploring each one. After tonight, they would do whatever was necessary to resume friendship.

But for now...

For now...

He moved languidly, enjoying the taste of her skin. He flicked his tongue over the delicate gold piercing in her navel. She'd gotten it while they were still in high school. It was the only rebellious thing she'd ever done, other than becoming friends with a nerdy kid like him.

He said, "I should buy you a ruby for here. Or a colored diamond, like what's in the earrings I gave you."

"No, you shouldn't."

"Why not?"

"Because it will only remind us of what we did tonight."

Damn, he thought. She was right. Giving her another jewel would be a mistake. "I won't do it. I won't buy you anything else." He thought about the cuff links she'd given him and the groomlike way they'd made him feel. "You can't buy me anything else, either."

She played with the ends of his hair. "I don't intend to."

"Good." He pushed her legs open and went down on her, kissing and licking and swirling his tongue.

She gasped and arched her hips, watching him through the misty light, telling him how much she liked it.

How good it felt.

How she never wanted it to end.

But it did end, with her shaking and shivering and coming all over his mouth.

She insisted on doing it to him, too, on giving him the same kind of lethal pleasure he'd just given her. He let her work her magic, his body responding in thick, hard greed.

But when it became too much for him to handle, he grabbed a condom, anxious to thrust inside.

He entered her, and they kissed warmly and fully, the sweetness of her lips drawing him deeper.

Locked together, they rolled over the sheets, and within no time, Lizzie was straddling him, her hair falling forward and framing her face. He gripped her waist as she traveled up and down, riding him quickly, fiercely.

They shifted again, bending and moving. He was behind her now, nibbling her neck and pumping like a stallion.

It didn't stop there. They swiveled onto their sides, kissed like crazy, then returned to where they'd begun, with Max braced above her.

Driving her toward a skyrocketing orgasm, he pushed her to the limit, making sure she came again.

And finally, *finally*, when she was in the throes of making primal sounds and clawing his back, he let himself fall.

Into the hot, hammering thrill of his wedding night.

In the morning, Lizzie awakened next to her husband. He was still asleep, the sheet bunched around his hips.

Should she gather her things and tiptoe off to her room? No, she thought. That would make her feel cheap, dashing down the hall, clutching her wedding gown.

The least she could do was find something to wear. She climbed out of bed and put on her panties. From there, she went to Max's giant walk-in closet, where his dresser was, and rummaged through the drawers.

The only belongings Lizzie had brought with her were in a suitcase that she'd left in her room. Later today, they were leaving on their honeymoon, jetting off to Nulah to start the adoption proceedings, and she wasn't moving into Max's mansion, not officially, until they got back.

She kept digging through his dresser, trying to decide what to borrow. Keeping it simple, she went for a black T-shirt and gray sweat shorts. She had to roll the waistband of the shorts down to her hips to make them fit, but it was better than just being in her panties. Rather than leave the hem of the T-shirt hanging, she twisted the material into a center knot and tied it below her bust.

Lizzie gazed at her reflection in the closet mirror, enjoying the way his clothes felt against her skin.

She frowned at her seductively smudged eye makeup and sleep-tousled hair. Nothing had changed in the light of day. She was still afraid of falling in love with him.

Determined to sneak off as quickly as she could, she exited his closet, hoping he remained asleep. But he was awake and was sitting up in bed.

He squinted at her. "What are you doing, pretty Lizard?"

"I borrowed some of your clothes." She stated the obvious, wishing her nickname didn't sound so endearing on his lips.

"So I see." He swept his gaze over her. "And how stylish you look in them, too."

While he studied her, she glanced at the scars on his chest, trapped in the memory of the well-intentioned touch he'd rebuffed. The solace he'd refused. She forced herself to look away from the scars, not wanting him to catch her doing it.

Would he rebuff her love, too? She hoped that she never had to find out.

He said, "I could use some breakfast. How about you?"

She wasn't the least bit hungry, but she replied, "Sure. I can fix it while you shower or whatever." She needed to bathe, too, but she wasn't ready to strip off her clothes. Or his clothes, as it were. She wanted to wear them a little longer.

"I'll shower after we eat." He got out of bed and took his tuxedo pants from the chair where he'd left them. Same chair where her dress was. "I can help you make the food."

He climbed into the pants, sans underwear. Of all things he could have worn this morning, he'd chosen to go commando in his wedding attire? He threw on the formal shirt, too, leaving it unbuttoned with the tails loose.

"No point in wasting a perfectly good suit," he said. "After all, I did buy the dang thing."

"Yes, you did." But most men wouldn't treat a pricey tuxedo as if it was casual gear. But Max wasn't most men.

He glanced toward his bathroom. "I'm going to brush my teeth before we go downstairs."

She tried for a smile. "So you can be minty fresh before breakfast? I should do that, too."

He smiled, as well. "I'll meet you in the kitchen."

When he was gone, Lizzie scooped up her gown, wrapping her shoes and stockings and jewelry inside it.

Once she was in her room, she deposited the bundle on her bed and went into her bathroom to brush her teeth. She washed her face, too, removing the remnants of her makeup. She also tamed her hair, taking a few minutes to get her emotional bearing.

Still wearing Max's clothes, she ventured downstairs and entered the kitchen. He was already there, removing pots and pans from cabinets. He had a carafe of coffee going, too.

She pitched in, and with minimal conversation they fixed ham, eggs and steel-cut oatmeal.

They sat across from each other at the main dining table, and Max drizzled honey over his cereal. Lizzie preferred hers with milk. But what struck her was how intently they were watching each other eat.

"Are you ready for our trip?" he asked.

Their big, fat, fake honeymoon, she thought. "Yes," she replied. "Are you?"

He nodded, but he didn't look any more ready than she was.

Since Nulah was twenty hours ahead of Los Angeles, Max and Lizzie arrived in time to hang out on the beach and swim in the crystal-blue sea. They tried to behave like newlyweds whenever other people were around. But mostly they kept to themselves, so they didn't have to make it harder than it already was. But either way, being in each other's company was absolute torture.

And so were their accommodations, Max thought.

Their bungalow was similar to the ones they'd stayed in before, with wonderful island amenities. The only difference this time was that they were sharing the same space.

Bedtime rolled around far too soon. Lizzie changed in the bathroom, putting on a long cotton nightgown. Max suspected it was the most modest thing she owned. But that didn't stop him from noticing how gracefully it flowed over her body.

"I can sleep on the couch," he said.

The couch was adjacent to the bed, as the main area of the bungalow was basically one big room. Even if he wasn't sleeping with her, he would be within tempting distance. But there was nothing either of them could do about that.

"All I need is a sheet," he said. "Sometimes I get hot when I sleep." He didn't mean "hot" in a sexual way, but it triggered sweet, slick memories of their wedding night.

Apparently for her, too. She shot him a dicey look.

A second later, she composed herself and removed the top sheet from the bed, gathering it for him. He took it from her, and she handed him a pillow, as well.

"We've got a big day ahead of us tomorrow," she said.

Max nodded. In the morning they would be going to the orphanage. "I hope Losa lets us see Tokoni. When I spoke with her earlier she said that she wasn't sure if we should see him on this trip."

Lizzie frowned. "Why not?"

"Typically she waits until the process is further along before she lets applicants spend more time with the child they are trying to adopt. She says it can get too emotional later if something goes wrong or if the applicants change their minds."

"We would never change our minds." She got into

bed, but she didn't lie down. She sat forward and pulled the covers over her legs.

"I know. But that's just how she does it."

He settled onto the couch, plumping the pillow behind him. Neither of them turned out the light. They gazed at each other from across the room. The windows were open, with a tropical breeze stirring the curtains.

"Why didn't you tell me this before now?" Lizzie asked.

"I didn't want to disappoint you. I know how badly you want to see Tokoni. How you were looking forward to his big, bright smile and giving him a hug. I want to do that, too."

Concern etched her brow, signaling another frown. "I hope she lets us see him. We've been waiting all this time."

"Yeah, planning a wedding, getting married. We've been to hell and back to become his parents." He made a tight face. "Sorry, that didn't sound very nice."

"I knew what you meant. It would have been so much easier if we could have stayed single and still adopted him."

"But that isn't how it worked out." He glanced down at his hand. "It's strange wearing a ring."

"You think you've got troubles?" She waggled her fingers, showing off her ruby. "Look at me, hauling this gigantic bauble around."

He laughed a little. "I'm surprised you didn't sink to the bottom of the ocean today."

A laugh erupted from her, too. "Good thing I didn't or you would've had to rescue me."

"Me performing CPR on you would have been a disaster." He smiled, winked, made another joke. "Mouth-to-mouth and all that."

She shook her head, and in the next uncomfortable instant, they both went silent. No more smiles. No more laughter. Their silly banter wasn't helping.

"We should try to sleep now," she said. "I just hope that I don't keep you awake, with the way I might be tossing and turning."

"I'm probably going to be restless, too." Being in the same room with her, knowing she was just a forbidden kiss away. But in the morning, they would get past it. Because all that mattered was doing what they'd come here to do.

To make Tokoni their son.

Lizzie and Max sat across from Losa in her office, but their meeting wasn't going well. Something didn't feel right, Lizzie thought. Even though she and Max had been prattling on about their wedding and how excited they were to adopt Tokoni, Losa seemed cautious of them.

In fact, she watched their every move, as if she were analyzing their body language. By now, Lizzie was so nervous that she kept glancing out the window, avoiding eye contact. Max seemed anxious, too. He shifted in his seat, like a kid who'd gotten called into the principal's office for committing a schoolyard crime.

Did Losa suspect that their marriage was a ruse? And if she did, why hadn't she said something before now? Why had she allowed them to continue the charade, letting them believe that they were being considered for the adoption?

Losa asked Lizzie, "Do you remember what I told you when you first interviewed me for your blog?"

"You told me a lot of things," she responded, getting more nervous by the minute. "I used a lot of it in the articles I wrote."

"Yes, you did. But what did I say about our guidelines and what's the most important character trait we look for in prospective parents?"

Lizzie's heart dropped to her stomach. "That they must be honorable people."

Max spoke up. "Are you questioning our character, Losa?"

The older woman turned toward him. "Yes, unfortunately, I am. When you first called me and said that you'd fallen in love and were getting married, I was concerned about the speed in which it seemed to be happening. But I gave you the benefit of the doubt, wanting to believe that your feelings were genuine and you weren't just playacting so you could adopt Tokoni."

Max's dark skin paled a little. But he said, "We're going to be the best parents we can be. We intend to devote the rest of our lives to Tokoni."

"Yes, but you don't intend to devote the rest of your lives to each other, do you?" She turned her attention to Lizzie. "I could tell from the moment you walked into my office today that you weren't a true bride. I know the difference between a happily married woman and one who is finding it difficult. You can barely look at your husband without having shadows in your eyes."

Lizzie gripped the edge of the desk. Not only were she and Max on the verge of losing Tokoni, but Losa was calling her out, baiting her to admit that the marriage wasn't real. But she couldn't do it. She couldn't say it out loud, not when she was so painfully afraid of falling in love with Max. "Please don't take Tokoni away from us."

"How can I allow you to adopt him," Losa replied, "when your actions haven't been honorable?"

Max interjected. "It isn't fair of you to say that."

"Isn't it?" Losa asked, challenging him to come clean. "Tell me, what were you going to do once the adoption was approved? Were you going to divorce your wife and create a broken home for your son? I want to know the truth, Max, and I want it now."

"All right," he said. "We are going to split up. But we aren't creating a broken home, not in the way you're implying. After the divorce, Lizzie and I planned to raise Tokoni in separate households, but we also planned to co-parent him with love and devotion. Both of us, together, as friends."

Losa blew out a heavy sigh. "That's not what Tokoni's mother wanted for him."

"I know." Max continued to defend their position. "But we couldn't bear to lose him, so we devised a way to make him our son. We can make the divorce work and still give Tokoni everything he needs."

Losa asked Lizzie, "Are you as certain about the divorce as Max is?"

Lizzie's grip on the desk tightened. She'd been wondering what it would be like to stay with her husband, to be the only woman in his life, and now she was being asked if dismantling their marriage was the right thing to do. She couldn't think, couldn't rationalize, not with him watching her from the corner of his eye. When he reached over, drawing her hand away from the desk and encouraging her to support the divorce, she knew that her worst fear had just come true.

That she loved him.

Absolutely, positively loved him.

What an awful time to figure it out, to see through the veil of her own heart. But she couldn't admit how she felt, not without destroying what was left of their friendship, so she lied and said, "Yes, I'm as certain about the divorce as he is."

Losa measured her. "So you honestly believe that it won't cause any problems later?"

"Yes," Lizzie lied again.

The older woman shook her head. "I'm sorry, but I disagree." She then told Max, "Neither of you is ready to be a parent."

His expression all but splintered. But in spite of his distress, Lizzie could tell that he wasn't giving up without a fight.

He said to Losa, "I understand how upset you

are about our deception, and I apologize for leading you on. But we are ready to be Tokoni's parents. We love him and believe that he's meant to be our son."

Losa adjusted her glasses. "I'm not denying that either of you loves the boy. I know you do." She spoke with strength and careful diction. "I wish things could be different, but I won't go against his mother's wishes or subject him to a broken home. There's another couple who's interested in him, and I'm going to consider their application in place of yours."

Oh, God. Lizzie pitched forward in her chair. Losa wasn't just denying their application. She was thinking of giving Tokoni to someone else.

"Who are they?" Max asked, firing a round of questions at her. "And how long ago did they apply? Do we know them? Are they someone who contacted you through our efforts to find Tokoni a home? Or are they a local couple?"

"I can't discuss them with you," Losa said. She sounded weary now, troubled that she was hurting Max and Lizzie, but determined to abide by her decision.

"Whoever they are, they won't be us," he said. He looked at Lizzie, his voice quaking. "They'll never be us."

She could see that his heart was breaking. Hers was, too. Everything inside her was shattering, cutting her in two.

Lizzie got up and ran out of the orphanage. Once she was outside, she burst into tears.

No child. No husband to keep. Only fractured love.

Max soon followed her. He wasn't crying. But he was shaking, his chest heaving through ragged breaths. He reached for her, and she collapsed in his arms.

More lost than she'd ever been.

Eleven

Feeling horribly, sickeningly numb, Max stared at the beach, where the sky met the sea, where peace and beauty were supposed to reign. But all he saw was emptiness.

He glanced over at Lizzie. She sat beside him on their bungalow deck, curled up in her chair, her knees drawn to her chest. After they'd left the orphanage, she'd dried her tears, but her eyes were still swollen, her mascara still softly smudged.

"We got married for nothing," he said, the hope of becoming a father crushed beneath the weight of his heart.

Her voice hitched. "Our wedding night didn't seem like nothing."

"No, but it was something we shouldn't have

done." The glittering warmth, the romance, the sex. Even now he longed to do it all over again, even if he knew it would only make matters worse. Taking fulfillment in Lizzie's body, holding her close, burying his face in her hair—none of those things was the answer. "We messed up." Mired in his grief, he kept looking at her. "If we hadn't slept together, we wouldn't have been so uncomfortable around each other, and then Losa wouldn't have figured us out."

Lizzie's voice hitched again. "She said that she was suspicious of us from the beginning."

"I know, but with the way we were acting, we gave ourselves away. We didn't seem like a real couple to her."

Still wrapped in the fetal position, she rocked in her chair. "We aren't a real couple."

"Everyone else believed that we were. Everyone except Losa." The person who had the power to take Tokoni away from them. "I can't believe that she turned us down. That Tokoni is never going to be ours. I wish she would have told us who the other applicants are. At least then—"

"We'd know who we're losing him to? How is that going to help?"

"I don't know. But they must be happily married or she wouldn't be considering them." He analyzed the strangers who might become Tokoni's parents. "What if their marriage breaks apart at some point? What if they end up divorced, too? It isn't fair that she's blaming us for not being in love. Who even knows what it means, anyway?"

A choked sound escaped from Lizzie's lips. "I don't want to talk about the definition of love."

"I'm just saying that—"

"Please, I can't do this..." She unfolded her arms and put her feet on the ground. Then, as quick as that, she ran toward the beach, on the verge of crying again.

Max's gut wrenched. Should he leave her alone? Or should he chase after her? He knew how fiercely she was hurting. He hurt, too, so damned badly.

He took a chance and headed toward her. She looked so lost, facing the water, the hem of her pale summer dress fluttering in the breeze. Was she blaming herself because Losa had put the initial burden on her? Did she think that she'd botched their phony presentation of love more than he had?

He came up behind her. The air smelled of salt and sea and sand, of tropical flowers and leafy foliage, of everything that reminded him of this trip they'd taken together. Their phony honeymoon, he thought.

"Lizzie?" He said her name, letting her know he was there.

She turned around, drew a breath. "Yes?"

He gently asked, "Do you think it's your fault because of what Losa said to you about not seeming like a true bride?"

She nodded. "Yes, but it's more than that, so much more."

"Tell me."

"I can't." Behind her, the ocean turned a foamy

shade of blue, rolling its way onto the picture-perfect shore.

"Yes, you can. I'm your BFF, remember? You can tell me anything."

"You won't understand."

"Yes, I will. You can confide in me." If not him, then who would she reveal herself to? "That's what we do, Lizzie. Tell each other our secrets."

"Then here it is. I want to be what Losa said I wasn't."

Too confused to make the connection, to let it sink in, he blinked at her. "That doesn't make sense."

"Yes, it does," she said, in a ghost of a whisper. "I want to be your true bride."

He shook his head, shook it so hard his brain rattled. "You don't know what you're saying. You're sad, you're agonizing over Tokoni, you're—"

"I'm in love with you, Max."

Recoiling from her words, he flinched. His mother used to tell him that she loved him after every beating, every cigarette burn, every painful punishment.

Trapped in his memories, he pushed his feet into the sand. Beneath the surface of the thick white grains, something pierced his skin. The edges of a broken shell, maybe. Or a tiny shard of glass or something else that didn't belong in a beach environment.

"I knew it was going to freak you out." Lizzie spoke quietly, cautiously. "It freaks me out, too. I was so afraid I was going to fall in love with you, and I did."

He snapped back into the conversation. "You've been afraid of this? For how long?"

"Since the day when you first showed me the garden."

Her deception punched him straight in the gut. "You've been stressing about this since before we got married, before you slept with me?"

"Yes. But I've been fighting my fears. On the night we were together, I prayed to survive it."

Max wasn't surviving it. Already he could feel the monsters coming to get him. The two-faced creatures lurking in the closet with the door barred shut.

"I think my fear of loving you is what Losa was seeing in my eyes," Lizzie said. "The shadows she mentioned. I doubt she knew that's why I didn't seem like a true bride, but she still sensed that something wasn't right."

Shadows, he thought. Monsters. He glanced up at the sun, then back at Lizzie. "My mother could have been her. *Anog Ite.*"

She squinted at him. "Double-Faced Woman?"

He nodded. The being who was condemned to wear two faces for seducing the *Wi*, the sun. He gestured to the sky. The setting sun was turning red, as if it was fused with fire, as bright as Lizzie's hair. "My mother had two faces. She was beautiful like *Anog Ite*, but ugly, too. Some people say that *Anog Ite* isn't evil. That she's just a figure of disharmony. But to me, she'll always be evil, like my mother, like the love she used against me."

"Love isn't evil, Max."

"No, but it makes people hurt." He reached out to touch Lizzie's hair. The beautiful redness. The fire. "Look what happened with Tokoni. We lost him, even though we loved him." He lowered his hand. "But maybe it's all just a smokescreen, this love that you think you feel for me. Maybe it isn't even real."

"It's real." Her voice broke. "What I feel is real."

"I don't think it is." He didn't want to believe it, couldn't let himself believe it. "You just think you love me because you got caught up in the fantasy of being a wife. But that's not you. You aren't the wifely type."

"My dad said that I was going to make a good wife."

"Your dad? He barely knows you. But I know you, Lizzie." He thumped a hand against his chest. "I know who you are."

"You don't know me anymore." She argued with him, defending the person she claimed to be. "I'm different. I'm changed."

He fought the urge to grab her, to shake her until she admitted that she didn't love him. But he wanted to hold her and kiss her, too. Max was a mess, more emotionally wrought than he'd ever been. "You were supposed to be my friend, my partner in parenthood. I trusted you."

"But you don't trust me now?"

"I don't know." He didn't know anything anymore.

"You can do whatever you want," she said. "But I'm going to pack my bags and catch the last boat to the mainland, before it gets dark."

He tried to stop her. "You don't have to do that."

"Yes, I do. I'll get a room on the mainland and take a commercial flight back to the States in the morning or whenever I can arrange it."

"I understand that you want to go back early. I do, too." The pretense of being on a honeymoon was over. "But we can take my jet and return together."

"What for? So you can keep trying to convince me that I don't love you? I need for you to believe me, to trust me." She turned and walked away, leaving him alone.

As he watched her go, he knew it was just a matter of time before the monsters reappeared.

Smothering him in the dark.

It took Lizzie three days to get a flight, and by then she suspected that Max was already home.

While riding in an airport limo, en route to her condo, she thought about the wedding dress she'd left in the guest room at his house. She couldn't bear for it to be in his possession.

So what was she going to do? Text him and ask him if she could come and get it? Oh, sure, she thought, just pop over to his mansion to collect her gown, as if there was nothing weird or painful or foolish about that.

Nonetheless, she did it. She fired off a text. Deep down, she knew this was just an excuse to see him. She could have sent a delivery service for the dress.

Max replied quickly, accepting her excuse and agreeing it was okay for her to stop by. But they didn't keep texting. Their communication was brief and choppy.

She gave the driver Max's address, and he plugged it into his GPS and headed for their new destination.

When they reached the security gate, Lizzie squeezed the handles on her purse, clutching the leather between her fingers, her nerves skittering beneath her skin.

After they were admitted onto the property, the car glided up the circular driveway and parked out front.

The chauffeur opened her door, and she said, "I won't be long. I just have to pick something up."

"Take all the time you need," he said.

What she needed was her husband to accept that she loved him. But she couldn't say that to the stranger who'd brought her here. So she merely smiled and thanked him. He was an older man, probably around her dad's age.

He returned to the limo, and she took the courtyard path to the front door. Lizzie rang the bell, trapped in a situation that she'd created. Was coming here a mistake? Or would it make things easier?

Max opened the door, and they gazed awkwardly at each other. He wore a pair of faded jeans with one of his prized *Star Wars* T-shirts. She almost smiled in spite of herself, but then she noticed the depiction was of Luke Skywalker battling Darth Vader, the latter with a bloodlike redness behind his black-helmeted eyes.

Good versus evil. Love versus pain.

"Come in," Max said.

Silent, she entered the mansion. She wanted to take him in her arms and make his pain go away. But she couldn't mend his ache, any more than she could cure her own.

She noticed that he was still wearing his wedding band. But she suspected that he was keeping up appearances and protecting his privacy, rather than face the questions people were going to throw at him if they saw him without his ring. He'd probably even told his pilot a phony story about why he'd returned from their honeymoon without her, citing a business emergency or something.

Lizzie hadn't taken off her ring yet, either. But she wanted to stay married. Her reason was better than his.

"I'll just go get my dress," she said, crossing the foyer and heading for the staircase.

He fell into step with her. "I'll go with you."

They made their way to the second floor, and once they reached the landing, she glanced in both directions, remembering the choice she'd made on their wedding night.

He appeared to be thinking the same thing. But neither of them said anything. They continued to the guest wing.

They entered the room where she'd left her dress. Her gown was on the bed, with the accessories that went with it, including the earrings Max had given her.

He stood off to the side, looking dark and brooding.

"It's as pretty as the day you wore it," he said,

about her dress. "With all its silk and lace and shiny beads." After a long pause, he added, "If everything hadn't gotten so messed up, you would have been moving into my house instead of dashing over here to grab your gown."

She wasn't running out the door yet. For now she was having a painful discussion with him. "Even if the adoption would have gone through, I would have left eventually with us getting divorced."

"That's what we agreed on."

"Until I bent the rules and fell in love with you?"

"It's not love, Lizzie. You just think it is."

"I can't see you again after this." It hurt too much to be near him, to keep hearing him deny her. "I shouldn't have even come here today." It was definitely a mistake.

He pulled a restless hand through his hair. "I know that we need to stay away from each other. But damn it, I'm going to miss you."

She couldn't begin to express how much she was going to miss him. She sat on the edge of the bed and touched a lace panel of her dress. "Nothing is ever going to be the same again."

He came forward and lifted one of the earrings, turning it toward the light. "Love was never supposed to be part of the deal. That's why our marriage and divorce was supposed to work."

But none of it had worked, not even the adoption. "When are you going to tell your family and friends about us?" Eventually he would have to remove his ring and face the music.

"I don't know. I just need a bit more time for now."

"Me, too." To hole up in her condo and cry. "When you're ready to deal with it, you can file for the divorce." She couldn't bring herself to end their marriage. They'd already lost the child who was supposed to be their son, and now they were losing each other, too. Just thinking about it made her want to crumble.

Turning away from him, she headed for the closet to retrieve the garment bag that had come with her wedding dress.

While he stood silently by, she placed everything inside the bag, zipping it up, shutting out the memory. The broken dream, she thought, of a marriage that never really was.

Max walked through his garden. He'd been spending countless hours here. He'd been going to the gym every night, too, but he always increased his workouts when he was stressed. Of course, immersing himself in plants and flowers was a whole other form of therapy. Or torture or whatever the hell it was.

Two weeks had passed since he saw Lizzie, since she collected her wedding dress, and he couldn't get her out of his mind. This was the worst era of his life, the absolute worst. And he'd been through some horrendous stuff when he was younger.

Yeah, he thought wryly, like the time his mom had abandoned him in their rathole of an apartment for three excruciating days. He'd survived on a half-empty box of cereal. No milk. No juice. No loving, caring parent. The TV had kept him company: cartoons in the morning, game shows in the afternoon, sitcoms and whatever else he could find that didn't scare him at night. Being alone was scary enough. And now he lived in a gigantic mansion, all by himself.

Hoorah for the nerd. The rich, single bachelor.

The monsters were back with a vengeance, just as he'd suspected they would be, keeping him awake at night, creeping and crawling into his brain. Hideous shadows in the dark. He couldn't shake them, no matter how hard he tried.

He kept walking through the garden, and as he approached the foliage that had been planted in honor of Tokoni, he stopped in midtrack. Mired in his loss, he wanted to pull every damned one of those plants out by their roots. But he would let them thrive instead, hoping and praying that Tokoni thrived in his new life, too. But it still tore him to shreds that the Creator had taken the boy away from him and Lizzie.

Lizzie. Elizabeth McQueen, his beautiful, faded friend. Even her name suggested her station in her life. She'd always been royalty, even before she'd become a high school homecoming queen or a grownup likeness to Lady Ari.

Why did she have to misconstrue her feelings into what she thought was love? Why did she have to fall into that kind of trap?

He strode over to the gazebo and went inside, thinking about the moment they'd first kissed. He envisioned her with that luscious red lipstick, her mouth warm and pliant against his.

He missed her beyond reason. But why wouldn't he? Normally when Max needed someone to ease him out of an emotional jam, he called her. She was his go-to, his dearest, closest friend, his comrade in arms. Sure, he had his brothers, but he always chose Lizzie first. He'd shared his secrets with her, things he'd never even talked to his brothers about. Garrett and Jake knew that Max had been abused as a kid, but he'd never opened up to them about it, not like he had with Lizzie. He'd told her everything, how it felt to be beaten and burned and scorned by his mother, how he used to cower in the closet, how he'd cried himself to sleep, but most of all, how his mother had insisted that she loved him.

Sharp, jagged, bloodthirsty love.

Lizzie knew that he'd never wanted to hear another woman say those words to him again. And now she claimed to love him, feeding the monsters and making his heart hurt from it.

Max twisted the ring on his finger, warning himself to remove it, to let Lizzie go, to divorce his wife, as soon as he could summon the willpower to do it.

Twelve

Lizzie couldn't stop thinking about Max, every minute of the day, every hour of the night.

She glanced at the microwave clock and saw that it was almost 7:00 p.m. On a Wednesday, she noted to herself. But that didn't matter because one day blurred into the next.

God, she was lonely without him.

She prepared a cup of hot tea and carried it into the living room. She hadn't been out of the house since they broke apart. But being a recluse wasn't all that tough. For food, she ordered groceries online and had them delivered. She'd had a few takeout meals brought over, too. But mostly, she didn't feel like eating.

Her dad, of all people, had texted her this morning. He'd wanted to know if she was back from her honeymoon and how the adoption proceedings had gone. Since she couldn't get away with another lie, she'd typed out the truth. Not in detail, but enough to convey that the adoption had fallen through, triggering a painful separation between her and Max.

She'd also told her father that she wanted to be alone. Not that he'd offered to rush over and comfort her. But she'd made it clear that she needed her space.

So far, there was no word from Max about the divorce. But she figured it was only a matter of time before he took legal action. Lizzie still hadn't removed the ruby and diamonds from her finger. For now she was still emotionally attached to being Max's wife, even if it was killing her inside.

She contemplated where he was at this early evening hour. She suspected that he was at the rough-and-tumble gym he frequented, letting off some steam. He took his workouts seriously, especially his boxing routines.

Her doorbell rang, and she nearly knocked over her tea. Was this the final countdown? Was it someone delivering the divorce papers? Was she being served?

She didn't want to answer it, but that would only prolong the inevitable. She opened the door, preparing for the worst.

Lizzie started. The person on the other side was her dad. What part of her needing to be alone didn't he understand?

"I just wanted to check on you," he said. He wore a dark gray business suit and a concerned expression.

She glanced away. "I'm okay. I'm handling it."

"You don't look okay."

If she broke down, would he know what to do or how to comfort her? She almost pitched forward, just to see if he would catch her. But she maintained her composure.

"This isn't necessary, Dad."

"Please, let me visit with you."

Lizzie gave in to his persistence, hoping it was going to be quick. Like a bullet to the head, she thought. The last thing she wanted was to feel like a sad and lonely child, longing for her daddy's affection.

"May I get you some tea?" she asked, playing the hostess, doing what came naturally. "I already brewed a cup for myself. Or I can make you coffee or something stronger, if you prefer." She knew that he sometimes enjoyed a martini after work.

"I'm fine, Elizabeth. I don't want anything."

"Then have a seat." She gestured to the sofa. He never called her Lizzie. That name had come from Mama.

They settled into the living room, and she clutched the armrests of her chair.

He asked, "What happened to cause all this? Why did the adoption fall through and why is it keeping you and Max apart?"

She'd already given him a condensed version in her texts, but that wasn't going to suffice, not face-to-face. So Lizzie took a deep breath and explained why she and Max had gotten married, how they'd lost Tokoni and why they were separated now, including the achy part about her falling in love with Max.

"I'm so sorry," her father said. "I never would have guessed that you weren't a true couple."

"Losa certainly figured it out."

"That's her job, I suppose, to be more observant than the rest of us. Maybe I didn't see through your charade because I always thought you were meant for each other."

She fought the threat of tears, forcing herself to keep her eyes clear and dry. "I'm never going to stop loving him."

"I never stopped loving your mother, either, even after she was gone." He paused, frowned, straightened his tie. "I just couldn't get over the loss."

"Mama dying was my loss, too."

"I know. And I should have been a better parent to you."

Yes, she thought. He should have. "Is that what you're trying to do now, Dad? Be an attentive parent?"

He nodded, making one last pull at the knot in his tie. "How I am doing so far?"

She managed a smile. Suddenly she was grateful that he was here, attempting to be the kind of father she'd always longed to have. "Pretty good, actually."

He blew out a relieved sigh. "Really?"

"Yes, really."

He finally smiled, too. "Did your mother ever tell you how she and I met?"

Curious, she shook her head. "No. No one ever told me."

"It was at a charity ball, a big, stuffy Savannah soiree. It was the first function of that type that I'd ever been to. My family was new money, nouveau riche, as they say, and this was an old-money crowd."

Lizzie leaned forward in her chair. "When was this? How old were you?"

"It was the summer before I left for university. Your mother was still in high school then, in her senior year at an all-girls' academy. That's who was hosting the ball. I was invited by a buddy of mine. He was dating one of the students and asked me to come along to meet her friend."

"And that friend was Mama?"

He nodded. "She was such a strange delight, the most eccentric person I'd ever known. We dated that summer, and even after I left for university, we stayed in touch. She used to write me the most fascinating letters. Later she went off to college, too, but we continued to correspond and see each other when we came home on breaks."

"When did you get engaged?"

"A year after she graduated. And two years later we were married. I wanted to wait until I was more established in my career. Her parents accepted me, but I still felt the new money stigma. They were such old-world people, so refined in their breeding. To me, they were like royalty."

"I wish I could have known them. And your parents, too."

"It was a tragedy that your mother and I shared, with both of us being only children and both of our families passing on so early in our lives—my father with heart failure when you were a baby, my mother with cancer when you were a toddler, and her parents in a helicopter crash, before you were even born. You'd think we were cursed."

Maybe they were, Lizzie thought. Being rich hadn't saved them, not old or new money.

He said, "Your mother never quite recovered from losing her parents. But she was already having bouts of depression before they died. It was always a part of who she was, being happy, then sad, then happy again. She had dramatic impulses, too, to do over-the-top things."

"Did you ever encourage her to seek help?"

"No. I thought that if I loved her enough, she would be okay. I didn't understand how depression worked. She might have been bipolar. Or maybe she had another type of disorder. I don't know. She never saw a doctor about it, so she was never diagnosed with anything."

Lizzie had to ask, "You never suspected that she was suicidal?"

His features tightened. "Sometimes she said odd things about death, about how freeing she thought it was going to be. But I didn't attribute that to her being suicidal." Another tight look came over him. "Even with as much as I loved her, sometimes she was just too much to handle. The moodier she got, the more time I spent at work." He lowered his head. "But I should have been there. I should have saved her."

Her heart went out to him, the father she'd barely known until now, the man struggling with his guilt. "You couldn't have, not without knowing how truly ill she was."

He glanced up. "If I'd gotten her the help she needed, she might be alive today."

"You can't go back and change it. You can only move forward."

"I'd like to do that, with you." He met her gaze. "But I have to admit that when you were a teenager and you brought Max home for the first time, I was impressed with how close you two seemed. I didn't know how to be a father to you, but he knew how to be your friend, just as you knew how to be his. It made me feel better, with him being part of your life."

Her emotions whirled, her breath lodging in her throat. "He went through some horrible things when he was a kid. Things he shared only with me, and now he's probably alone with his turmoil. He doesn't confide in people very easily, not even his brothers."

"If that's the case, then don't you think he needs you? More than he's ever needed you before?"

Yes, she thought. Heavens, yes. This wasn't the time to give up on Max. Even if he refused to believe that she loved him, she could still do what she'd always done.

Be his friend.

* * *

Max had been at the gym for hours, trying to knock the crap out of his past, throwing power punches at a heavy bag.

Why couldn't he let go of what his mother had done to him? Why did those memories have to be there, lurking in the dark? He should be better than that; he should be stronger than the monsters.

As he threw another punch, a warm, hazy feeling came over him. He sensed a presence behind him.

An immortal, he thought, a spirit helper. The Lakota called them *Tunkasila*. Although it translated to Grandfather, it applied to all guardians. In that regard, the term was genderless. Sprit helpers came in many forms, and he could tell that his guardian was female. He could feel her whisper-soft energy.

Max had never seen one before. None had ever appeared to him. But now a guardian was here, offering to help him banish the monsters, to get rid of them for good.

He turned around, startled by what he saw. His guardian looked just like Lizzie: bright blue eyes, long, fiery red hair.

Confused, he shook his head. Had a spirit helper borrowed her form? Or was it Lady Ari dressed in street clothes? Had *Tunkasila* called upon her to intervene?

He felt as if he were in the middle of a dream. Maybe he was. Maybe he wasn't even at the gym at all.

She moved a little closer, this beautiful, oddly alluring spirit who mimicked Lizzie.

"I'm sorry I didn't call," she said. "But I figured you'd be here, so I came on over."

He blinked, told himself to get a grip. The female standing before him wasn't an immortal. She was flesh and blood. She was human. She *was* Lizzie.

Tunkasila help him, he thought. He longed to pull her into his arms, to tell her how miserable he'd been without her. But he stood motionless instead, dripping with sweat, still wearing his boxing gloves. What if he touched her, what if he held her and the monsters still didn't go away?

He glanced down, taking a quick inventory of her hand. She was wearing her wedding ring. So was he, under his left glove.

"My dad came to see me," she told him.

Max finally spoke. "He did? When?"

"Today. This evening. We had a meaningful conversation, mostly about my mother. But he stopped by to make sure I was all right. He knows that you and I aren't together anymore." Her gaze lingered on him. "I'm sorry for taking my friendship away from you."

"Are you offering to be my friend again?"

She nodded. "Yes."

"Even if we get divorced?"

She nodded again, tender, determined, true. "I'll be your friend, no matter what."

He glanced at her ring again and noticed that her nail polish was chipped. He'd never seen her without a flawless manicure before. It made her seem fragile, but somehow powerful, too. "You'd do that to yourself? You'd deliberately put yourself in a painful situation for me?"

"I can't turn my back on you. I love you too much to do that."

His heart thumped in his chest. She wasn't *Tunkasila*. But she was still his guardian, his helper. He removed his gloves, setting them aside.

He held out his hand to show her his ring. "I couldn't bear to take it off. I haven't filed the papers yet, either. I kept telling myself that I should, but I just couldn't bring myself to do it." He studied her, with her gauzy blouse and long, floral-printed skirt. He appreciated how it looked on her. Flowers were becoming her signature to him. He imagined them raining down from the ceiling like petals from the gods. "Since we split up, I must have walked through the garden at my house a hundred times, going into the gazebo and thinking about our wedding. It's been torture, Lizzie, not having you in my life."

She reached for him. "I'm here now."

As soon as he hugged her, her blouse stuck to his bare skin. "I'm getting you all sweaty."

"I don't care." She held him tighter. "It feels good."

"I'm sorry for punishing you for loving me, for turning a deaf ear to it. But you know how badly it scared me."

She stepped back to look at him. "I'm not trying to push you into more than you're ready for."

"I know. But I want to be ready. I want to stop being afraid of love, to accept that I'm worthy of it." He explained the feelings rattling around inside him. "Whenever my mother used those words, they diminished me, as if I didn't deserve to be loved. They made me feel small and insignificant. A shell of the boy I was, of the man I was going to be. But that's not what you're doing. That's not what love is."

She touched his cheek, skimming her fingers along the hollowed area beneath the bone. "This is a huge step for you. For both of us." Tears welled in her eyes. "I love you, Max."

For the first time in his life, he wanted to hear a woman say those words to him. But in this case, she wasn't just any woman. She was his wife. "I love you, too," he said. He knew now that he did. That maybe somewhere in the depths of his angst-ridden soul, he always had loved her.

She kissed him, creating a fusion of warmth and comfort and strength. If the monsters tried to come back, Max would slay them. He would slice them to bits, with his guardian by his side.

Lizzie wasn't an immortal, but *Tunkasila* had sent her to him just the same. She'd been there all these years. The friend he needed, the lover he craved, the fiery-haired, tender, loving, supportive partner who'd turned his heart around.

When the kiss ended, he took both of her hands and held them in his. "There's something we need to do, besides resume our marriage."

"We have to try to get Tokoni back," she replied, clearly aware of where his mind was at.

He nodded. "Even if Losa already started processing the other couple's application, we have to try. It's only been a few weeks. There's still time for her to change her mind."

"What if she won't budge?"

"Then we'll have to keep trying. We can't give up, Lizzie. Tokoni is a part of us. He belongs to us as much as we belong to each other."

"Yes, he does." She put her head against his shoulder. "We're supposed to be a family, the three of us."

"I'll call Losa and make the arrangements for us to go to Nulah as soon as we can." He wrapped his arms around her. "But for now I want to take you home with me." And be together, he thought, as husband and wife.

Lizzie stripped off her clothes, her heart reeling. Max loved her the way she loved him. He'd said it openly, with a truth she'd seen in his eyes. And now they were in the master bath at his house. He hadn't showered at the gym. But she was glad that he'd waited, so they could get cleaned up together.

Clean and naked and wet.

He adjusted the water temperature, and she joined him in the clear glass enclosure. There was plenty of room for two people. But to her, it felt warm and cozy.

He took her in his arms, and they stood that way for the longest time, just holding each other, letting the water rain over them.

As steam fogged up the glass, Lizzie turned to face the enclosure door and drew a Valentine-type heart on it, using the tip of her finger. With a look of fascination, Max added their initials.

$M + L$, in his masculine script.

She smiled, laughed a little, felt her own heart go bump. "How wonderfully teenage of us."

"We're making up for lost time. Or I am, anyway. I still can't believe you had a crush on me when we were kids."

"Just like you had trouble believing that my love was real?"

"I believe it now." He kissed her, strong and deep, his tongue making its way into her mouth.

Her body flexed, her mind swirled. She pulled him closer, the taste of passion between them. The kiss went on and on.

And on some more.

Finally, when they came up for air, she realized that her eyes were still closed. She opened them, water dotting her lashes.

Max pumped liquid soap into his hands and began washing her breasts. He thumbed her nipples, making them peak from his warm, slick, sudsy touch.

Sweet love. Sweet marriage.

Lizzie relished every wondrous thing he was doing to her. "I like the scent of your soap." The sandalwood that often lingered on him.

"And I like touching you this way."

He bathed her entire body, front to back. He washed her hair, too, with his shampoo. Everything in the shower belonged to him, including her.

He massaged her scalp, his fingers kneading her

skin. She'd always enjoyed going to the salon, but this, this…

He used a conditioner, then moved out of the way, encouraging her to step under the spray so she could rinse, completing the task herself. But it didn't end there. He watched her, like a voyeur taking forbidden thrills.

Within a heartbeat, he came forward, kissing her again. She nearly lost her breath, especially when he dropped to his knees. She gazed down at him, and he glanced up at her, a carnal warning in his eyes.

Lizzie didn't know if she was going to make it out of this situation alive. He used his mouth in wicked ways, relentless in his pursuit—an intense journey, hot and thorough.

The orgasm that rocked her body sent her into a state of erotic shock. She moaned in the midst of it.

"Max… Max… Maxwell…"

She rarely used his full name, but she was doing it now, slipping into the sound of it. She gripped his shoulders to keep from falling over, her knees going weak, her pulse thumping in intimate places.

In the afterglow, he stood and smiled, obviously pleased by what he'd done to her. Then, leaving her staring after him, he lathered his own body and washed his own hair.

As the steam thickened, she blinked through the haze. Her husband looked like a modern-day god, a contemporary warrior, every muscle in its place.

Needing him more than ever, she approached him. As she moved into his arms, he obliged her, pulling her tight against him. She wedged a hand between their bodies. He was already half-hard.

Lizzie took it all the way, giving him a full-blown erection with a rhythm that rippled through both of them.

He grabbed the condom that he'd brought into the shower and tore into it. She was just as eager, just as wanting.

Having sex while standing up wasn't an easy feat, but they managed just fine—in lip-biting, nail-clawing, body-twisting ways.

He rasped, "If we weren't already married, I would ask you to marry me, right now, just like this."

"And I would say yes." A thousand, hard-driving, hip-thrusting times yes.

They feasted on each other, mating like animals. Max came in a burst of male heat, and Lizzie held him while he shuddered, held him until she lost the battle and exploded into a soul-shattering orgasm, too.

Seconds passed before either of them had the stamina to move. When they did, it was to put their foreheads together and glance over at the mist-drawn heart.

Although it was melting, dripping down the glass, the sentiment remained.

M + L. Forever.

Thirteen

Three days later, Max and Lizzie arrived in Nulah, ready to fight for the adoption. Losa agreed to see them and hear what they had to say, but, as usual, she wasn't making any promises.

On this summer afternoon, they gathered in the picnic area of the orphanage. The sun was shining, with a fresh, clean, grassy scent in the air.

None of the kids were outside. Max wished they were. He was desperate for a glimpse of Tokoni. He knew Lizzie was, too.

She sat next to him, with Losa seated across from them, a wooden tabletop between them.

Max decided to start the conversation with an emotional tone since that's how he was feeling. "I love my wife," he told Losa. "And she loves me. She loved me on the day you denied our application, but she was struggling with her feelings then."

The older woman squinted beneath her glasses, narrowing her gaze at him. "This better not be another fake attempt at trying to make me think you're a couple."

"It's real." He reached for Lizzie's hand and held it, threading his fingers through hers. "We're not pretending to be together. We *are* together. On the day our application was denied, we returned to the resort where we were staying and had a breakdown. But it was worse for Lizzie because she admitted that she loved me, and I turned her away."

Lizzie didn't interject. She remained silent, listening to him recount their story. Losa was listening, too.

Max continued. "I was afraid of being loved by Lizzie, afraid of hearing her say those words. It relates back to my childhood and the terrible things my mother did to me."

Losa didn't reply. But she was no longer squinting at Max. Her expression had softened. Of course she already knew that he'd come from an abusive environment. He'd mentioned it when he first volunteered at the orphanage, but not to the degree he was speaking of it now.

He went on to say, "I accepted being loved by other people. My foster brothers love me, and I love them. I love Tokoni, too. That kid has been part of me since the moment I met him." He glanced at his wife, and she squeezed his hand, giving him her support.

"But it was different with Lizzie because she knew all my secrets. When we were teenagers, I told her every painful detail, things I never told anyone else. That brought us together as friends. But now that I'm able to look back on it, I think it created a wall between us, too. I built that wall around other women, as well, insisting that I was incapable of falling in love. Yet all along, I think I was having those types of feelings for Lizzie, even though I was too mixed up to recognize them." He paused, giving himself a second to breathe. "I'm sorry if this sounds like psychobabble, but it's the only way I know how to describe it."

"I understand," Losa said. "We have children here who've been abused. I know how it can affect them. But we do everything in our power to get them the help they need."

"That didn't happen for me. I got lost in the foster care system, with social workers who were overwrought with work, with caseloads they couldn't handle. But I was glad that they left me alone. I didn't want to be singled out. Once my brothers took me under their protective wings, I felt a little better. But I was still guarded. I've always been that way." He turned toward the beautiful redhead by his side. "But not anymore."

Lizzie scooted even closer to him. "Max isn't the only one who's been working through his issues. I was just as afraid of loving him as he was of loving me. Those are the shadows you saw in my eyes the last time we were here." She softly added, "But I'm stronger now, and I'm ready to be a wife and mother."

Max quickly added, "You were right when you told us before that we weren't ready to be Tokoni's parents. We deceived you and ourselves in our effort to adopt him, but now we want to do it in the right way. We love Tokoni, and we want the opportunity to make him our son, to devote ourselves to him and each other." He implored her. "Will you consider our application in place of the other couple you told us about? Will you give us a chance?"

Losa didn't reply. She only shifted in her seat.

Max hurriedly said, "I guarantee that everything we just told you is true. But if you want us to sign an affidavit to attest to our feelings, we will. We'll sign it in blood if we have to."

"You don't need to go that far." Losa removed her glasses, cleaning them on the hem of her blouse. She put them back on and sighed. "I have a confession to make." A beat later, she said, "I lied to you about the other couple. They aren't real. They don't exist."

Max jerked his head in surprise. Lizzie did, too.

Losa explained, "I was concerned that if you thought Tokoni was still available, it would be harder for you to move on with your lives. I didn't want you holding on to false hope. Also, it was easier to deceive you once I surmised that you were deceiving me." She frowned. "I'm not prone to lies. That isn't my nature, and I'm sorry I used that tactic on you. You deserved the truth from me, just as I deserved it from you."

Max's thoughts spun inside his head: relief, confusion, new hope. Beside him, Lizzie's hand began to tremble. Their fingers were still interlocked.

He asked Losa, "Is this your way of telling us that you're reconsidering us for the adoption, that we have a chance? Or are you just making amends for deceiving us?"

"Both," she replied, her frown morphing into a smile. "You told me everything I needed to hear, and now I'm able to look past your former lies and see the love and care and devotion between you. The kind of devotion Tokoni's mother wanted his adoptive parents to have."

Lizzie burst into a grateful sob, and Max thanked Losa and drew his wife into his arms, inhaling the sweet scent of her skin, this beautiful, perfect woman who was going to be the mother of his child.

He turned back to Losa. "May we see Tokoni? Just for a minute or so? You don't have to tell him that we're going to adopt him. You can wait until we've been approved." Max knew that he and Lizzie still had a ton of paperwork ahead of them. "But it would be wonderful if we could at least visit with him."

Losa smiled again. "I think that would be all right. I'm certain that he's going to be as thrilled to see you as you are to see him." Short and stout, she came to her feet and moved away from the bench. "Stay here, and I'll bring him to you."

Max and Lizzie waited together, holding hands, anxious to see their boy. Nearly three months had passed since the last time they saw him, but it seemed like an eternity.

When they spotted him crossing the lawn with Losa, they stood and exchanged a smile. He was just as they remembered him, with his bangs flopping across his forehead and a wide grin splitting across his face. The older woman let Tokoni go, and he raced through the grass, heading for Max and Lizzie.

They knelt to greet him, and Tokoni barreled straight into them. The three of them toppled to the ground, arms and legs akimbo. Peals of laughter ensued, rumbling into breathless, mindless joy.

Max helped Lizzie up and pulled Tokoni toward them for a group hug: this crazy, beautiful family in the making.

After leaving the orphanage and returning to the island where they'd stayed before, Lizzie enjoyed a cozy evening with her husband. This was the trip of a lifetime and the original honeymoon they should've had.

For dinner, they ordered room service. And now that they'd finished their meals, they shared a dessert designed for two: a fruit tart, smothered in vanilla cream and laden with kiwis, bananas, berries and figs. They ate from the same plate, both with their own fork.

Lizzie gazed admiringly at her man. He sat cross-legged on the bed, wearing nothing but a pair of boxer-briefs. She was in her underwear, too. It just seemed like the thing to do on this warm summer night.

"What an amazing day," he said.

She nodded her agreement. "Yes, it was. But I can't wait until the day comes when we can bring Tokoni back to the States with us. Can you imagine how excited he's going to be?"

Max smiled and dipped in to the tart. "He'll be able to finish the drawings in his booklet, filling in the color of his parents' hair. His mother is going to be a beautiful redhead, and his father is going to have black hair."

"His gorgeous father, you mean."

He smiled again. "If you say so."

"I do." She took a creamy, fruity bite and moaned. Then she laughed and covered her mouth. "This is so darned good. I probably have it all over my face."

"You don't, actually. But it kind of reminds me of feeding you our wedding cake and kissing it off your lips. That was the sexiest thing I've ever done in a room full of people."

She suspected that this dessert session was headed in a sexy direction, too. That once they finished pigging out on the tart, they would be kissing like mad. But for now she asked, "What happened to the top tier of our cake?"

"I don't know. What's supposed to happen to it?"

"There's a tradition where brides and grooms freeze it and then eat it on their first anniversary."

"If that's the case, then the chef or someone in the catering staff probably kept it for us, putting it in the freezer in the ballroom kitchen."

She hoped they did. "We'll have to check when

we get home. It would be fun celebrating with you next year with our cake."

As Max speared his next bite, some of the crust crumbled onto his lap. He grinned, shrugged it off. "You know what I love, besides you?"

"What?" she asked, mesmerized by him.

"I love hearing you refer to the mansion as home. I love that my place is your home now, too."

She leaned over and nabbed another forkful. "I wonder what Tokoni is going to think of it. I'll bet he's going to be overwhelmed with how big it is."

"Once we're able to tell him about the adoption, we should show him pictures of it so he knows ahead of time where he'll be living."

"I hope the adoption goes quickly." Lizzie was anxious for them to become Tokoni's parents, to make that dream come true.

"It could happen as quickly as three months. We could have him home by Halloween. That could be our first official holiday, with the three of us together."

She glanced toward the window, where an ocean breeze was stirring. "Do they celebrate Halloween here?"

"I don't think so. But once we take the online classes that are required for the adoption, we'll know a lot more about how to blend Tokoni's traditions with ours." He shifted his legs, keeping them crossed, but moving his knees a little. "Remember when we talked about bringing Tokoni back for vacations so he can visit his homeland? I was thinking we should take it a step further and buy a summer house in Nulah."

"I love that idea. Maybe we can find a home near the orphanage, so Tokoni can play with the other kids and we can volunteer our time."

"That sounds good to me." He polished off his section of the tart. "Maybe, at some point, we could even adopt more kids."

Oh, wow. Lizzie widened her eyes. "You want more children?"

"Sure. Why not? If we're going to be a family, then we might as well share the love. We could adopt them from here and from the States, too, from foster care. Is that okay with you, to have more kids?"

"I hadn't thought about it until now. But yes, I would love to have a big family with you." She imagined them with a house full. "I think it would thrill Tokoni, too, to have siblings to call his own, to be part of something so meaningful."

"Then it's a deal. A future plan." He watched her take the last bite of the tart.

As she licked a dollop of the cream filling off her lips, he took the empty plate away, along with their forks. Was he preparing for the fast, mad kissing?

Once the area was clear, Max nudged her onto the bed. But he didn't rush her into it. He took his time, kissing her languidly, making her sigh like the dreamy new bride that she was.

He was warm and giving, gentle and passionate. There was no reason to hurry, she realized. No reason to get frantic on this soft, sweet island day. They had all the time in the world to be together.

She ran her hands over his body, over his scars, over the pain from his past. He looked into her eyes without the slightest flinch.

He caressed her, peeling off her bra and panties. Naked, with her heart fluttering, she moaned from the pleasure. The foreplay was as light and breezy as the ocean air.

He ditched his underwear and climbed on top of her. She felt the beats of his heart, tapping against her own.

He used protection, and they made love in a stream of consciousness, of tender awareness, with him being deep inside her. Deep, deep inside, just where she wanted him.

They moved in unison, her body becoming part of his, rolling over the bed, kissing as they tumbled. Lizzie had never had sex this magical before. But she was with Max, her husband, her dearest friend, the man she'd known for nearly half of her life.

He rocked his hips, filling her up, sliding back down, creating a motion that took her to the edge—and beyond.

Lizzie came, shuddering in silky warmth. And so did Max. She felt him, falling, drifting, spilling into her.

At the very same time.

The adoption was final in mid-October, and now it was Halloween, the holiday Lizzie and Max had talked about.

With the joy of motherhood in her heart, Lizzie studied the people that surrounded her. Jake and Carol were here with their daughter and Garrett and Meagan with theirs. Everyone gathered in the living room of the mansion, preparing to take the kids trick-or-treating.

Tokoni was dressed as a superhero, and he looked darned fine in his red-and-blue outfit and fly-through-the-air cape. Lizzie's mind drifted back to the first day she'd met him in the library of the orphanage. She'd told him that she was writing an article about the kids there, and he'd asked her then if he could be a superhero in her story.

And now he was. Lizzie had her very own superhero son.

She smiled at him, then glanced at her husband. He was as excited as she was. Tokoni had transitioned beautifully into their lives. He loved being their child and living in his big, fancy home in America. Halloween was new and exciting for him, too. Already, he adored sharing the spotlight with his cousins.

Ivy was costumed as a fairy, with glitter and sequins and colorful prettiness. Only she called herself an "Ella" instead of a "fairy." Meagan explained that it was because Ivy had a toy fairy, a tiny statue, named Ella, which also meant fairy. But it meant more than that to Meagan. When she was a child, she'd had a baby sister named Ella who'd died of SIDS. An angel in heaven.

Speaking of angels...

Nita was dressed as an angel, in a frilly white dress with gossamer wings. She was ten months old now and holding on to tables to walk. She babbled, too, in pre-toddler speak, saying things that no one understood except her. She was a darling child, a combination of her mother and father.

"I guess it'll be my sworn chocolate duty to eat her candy," Jake said as he caught Lizzie admiring his little angel. "Since she's too young for it."

"Yeah," Garrett chimed in. "That's probably just what the devil himself would do."

Jake flashed a mischievous grin. He sported a shiny red tuxedo and a set of pointy horns. He was the only parent out of the bunch who'd gotten dressed up. "Nita likes my costume."

Carol laughed. "That's just because she knows her daddy has always been a bit of a demon."

Lizzie couldn't ask for a nicer group of people. She loved Max's family. They were her family now, too, hers and Tokoni's.

She walked over to Max. "My dad is coming by later," she told him. "After we get back from trick-or-treating."

"Really? That's great." He leaned into her. "I'm glad he's taking the time to get to know Tokoni."

"I think he wants to learn to be a grandpa."

"He's welcome to see Tokoni anytime. Besides, we're going to keep him busy with the brood we're going to adopt. Just think of how many superheroes there will be around here in the future. And whatever else they decide to be."

Lizzie nodded, turning to look at the kids who were here today, pleased with how happy all of them were. They sat in a circle on the floor, all with their own plastic jack-o'-lantern candy bucket. Halloween was fast becoming her favorite holiday. But Christmas was going to be spectacular, too. She couldn't wait for it to arrive.

Jake adjusted his horns and asked, "So, is it time to get this show on the road?"

"Definitely." Max dashed over to Tokoni and picked him up. He spun him around, making him fly. "We're ready."

Yes, they were, Lizzie thought, as their son squealed in delight. They were ready.

For everything.

* * * * *

*Don't miss the first two Billionaire Brothers
from Sheri WhiteFeather!*
BILLIONAIRE BROTHERS CLUB:
*Three foster brothers grow up, get rich...
and find the perfect woman.*

*WAKING UP WITH THE BOSS
SINGLE MOM, BILLIONAIRE BOSS*

Available now from Harlequin Desire!

And you'll also love Sheri WhiteFeather's moving
FAMILY RENEWAL *series...*

*LOST AND FOUND FATHER
LOST AND FOUND HUSBAND
THE BACHELOR'S BABY DILEMMA
COMING HOME TO A COWBOY*

Available from Harlequin Special Edition!

* * *

*If you're on Twitter, tell us what you think of
Harlequin Desire! #harlequindesire.*

SPECIAL EXCERPT FROM

HARLEQUIN Desire

Their weekend in Milan led to a child, but after an accident, rich jeweler Jaeger Ballantyne can't remember any of it! Now Piper Mills is back in his life, asking for his help, and once again he can't resist her...

Read on for a sneak peek at
HIS EX'S WELL-KEPT SECRET,
the first in Joss Wood's
***BALLANTYNE BILLIONAIRES** series!*

She had to calm down.

She was going to see Jaeger again. Her onetime lover, the father of her child, the man she'd spent the past eighteen months fantasizing about. In Milan she hadn't been able to look at him without wanting to kiss him, without wanting to get naked with him as soon as humanly possible.

Jaeger, the same man who'd blocked her from his life.

She had to pull herself together! She was not a gauche girl about to meet her first crush. She had sapphires to sell, her house to save, a child to raise.

Piper turned when male voices drifted toward her, and she immediately recognized Jaeger's deep timbre. Her skin prickled and burned and her heart flew out of her chest.

"Miss Mills?"

His hair was slightly shorter, she noticed, his stubble a little heavier. His eyes were still the same arresting blue, but his shoulders seemed broader, his arms under the sleeves of the black oxford shirt more defined. A soft leather belt was threaded through the loops of black chinos.

The corner of his mouth tipped up, the same way it had the first time they'd met, and like before, the butterflies in her stomach crashed into one another. She couldn't, wouldn't throw herself into his arms and tell him that her mouth had missed his, that her body still craved his.

He held out his hand. "I'm Jaeger Ballantyne."

Yes, I know. We did several things to each other that, when I remember Milan, still make me blush.

What had she said in Italy? *When we meet again, we'll pretend we never saw each other naked.*

Was he really going to take her statement literally?

Jaeger shoved his hand into the pocket of his pants and rocked on his heels, his expression wary. "Okay, skipping the pleasantries. I understand you have some sapphires you'd like me to see?"

His words instantly reminded her of her mission. She'd spent one night with the Playboy of Park Avenue and he'd unknowingly given her the best gift of her life, but that wasn't why she was here. She needed him to buy the gems so she could keep her house.

Piper nodded. "Right. Yes, I have sapphires."

"I only deal in exceptional stones, Ms. Mills."

Piper reached into the side pocket of her tote bag and hauled out a knuckle-size cut sapphire. "This exceptional enough for you, Ballantyne?"

Don't miss
HIS EX'S WELL KEPT SECRET by Joss Wood,
available April 2017 wherever
Harlequin® Desire books and ebooks are sold.

And follow the rest of the Ballantynes with
REUNITED…AND PREGNANT, available June 2017,
Linc's story, available August 2017,
and Sage's story, available January 2018.

www.Harlequin.com

Whatever You're Into… Passionate Reads

Looking for more passionate reads from Harlequin®?
Fear not! Harlequin® Presents, Harlequin® Desire and
Harlequin® Blaze offer you irresistible romance stories
featuring powerful heroes.

HARLEQUIN *Presents.*

Do you want alpha males, decadent glamour and jet-set
lifestyles? Step into the sensational, sophisticated world of
Harlequin® Presents, where sinfully tempting heroes ignite a
fierce and wickedly irresistible passion!

HARLEQUIN *Desire*

Harlequin® Desire novels are powerful, passionate and
provocative contemporary romances set against a backdrop of
wealth, privilege and sweeping family saga. Alpha heroes with
a soft side meet strong-willed but vulnerable heroines amid a
dramatic world of divided loyalties, high-stakes conflict and
intense emotion.

HARLEQUIN *Blaze*

Harlequin® Blaze stories sizzle with strong heroines and
irresistible heroes playing the game of modern love and lust.
They're fun, sexy and always steamy.

Be sure to check out our full selection of books
within each series every month!

www.Harlequin.com

Turn your love of reading into rewards you'll love with

Harlequin My Rewards

**Join for FREE today at
www.HarlequinMyRewards.com**

Earn **FREE BOOKS** of your choice.

Experience **EXCLUSIVE OFFERS** and contests.

Enjoy **BOOK RECOMMENDATIONS** selected just for you.

PLUS! Sign up now and get **500** points right away!

Earn **FREE** REWARDS
HarlequinMyRewards.com
Join Today!

MYR16R

HARLEQUIN®

A *Romance* FOR EVERY MOOD™

Love the Harlequin book you just read?

Your opinion matters.

Review this book on your favorite book site, review site, blog or your own social media properties and share your opinion with other readers!